Phoebe swayed on her feet, suddenly dizzy from the blow to her head. She sank to her knees and double over with nausea.

Closing her eyes, she willed the physical symptoms of a delayed stress reaction to pass as the horrifying vision replayed in her mind.

Wisps of mist drift across damp, moss covered stones, like ghosts mocking the fading fog . . . The glint of defiance in Paige's eyes as a Darklighter arrow pierces her heart, death instant and not a lingering agony . . .

Phoebe gagged, wishing she could erase the terrible images. If the vision came to pass, Todd would kill Paige, the scarred Darklighter would kill the boy, and he would transform into a teenaged Darklighter and kill Leo. The presence of the symbolic mist meant that the outcome could still be changed.

But time was running out.

D0434725

More titles in the

Pocket Books series

All Pocket Books are available by post from:
Simon & Schuster Cash Sales. PO Box 29
Douglas, Isle of Man IM99 1BQ
Credit cards accepted.
Please telephone 01624 836000
fax 01624 670923
Internet http://www.bookpost.co.uk
or email: bookshop@enterprise.net for details

MIST AND STONE

An original novel by Diana G. Gallagher

Based on the hit TV series created by

Constance M. Burge

POCKET
BOOKS

LONDON • SYDNEY • NEW YORK • TOKYO • SINGAPORE • TORONTO

First published in Great Britain in 2003 by Pocket Books.
An imprint of Simon & Schuster UK Ltd.
Africa House, 64–78 Kingsway, London WC2B 6AH

Originally published in 2003 by Simon Pulse,
an imprint of Simon & Schuster Children's Division, New York

A CIP catalogue record for this book is available from the British Library

ISBN 07434 62491

3 5 7 9 10 8 6 4

Printed by Cox & Wyman Ltd, Reading, Berkshire

To Andrea Haag,
with affection and gratitude
for her support and help
in making this book possible

Chapter

1

Piper dropped an armful of kneepads, winter gloves, hats, and a cycle helmet on the bed. She blew a strand of chronic flyaway hair off her forehead and stared at the miscellaneous junk and valuables she had pulled out of the closet. She decided to sort everything into "toss," "keep," and "store" piles later, after the closet was emptied.

Over the past few months, Piper had thrown out a few things, but she hadn't been able to completely break the Halliwell pack rat habit. Most of her old clothes and mementos had been packed and stored in the attic, which seemed to generate extra nooks and crannies as needed. There was always room for another trunk, suitcase, or box. Still, she and Leo both owned a lot of stuff they needed to access on a regular basis. So after months of trying to jam the belongings

1

of two into storage space intended for one, Leo was finally going to install an organizer.

"Leo definitely got the better end of the deal," Piper mumbled. "He's shopping, and I've got disaster management."

Piper sighed as she surveyed the mess left in the closet. Clothes had fallen off hangers, and various shoes and boots—some in pairs and some not—were strewn across the floor. Dust balls clung to an assortment of dirty socks that had been missing for months. Several boxes sat precariously close to the edge of a sagging, single shelf. Spiders ranging in size from tiny to too-big-for-comfort fled meticulously spun webs for the safety of dark corners.

"You guys better run," Piper sputtered as she wiped a wisp of web off her nose. "I haven't vanquished a demon in days, and I've got itchy freeze fingers."

Actually, Piper thought as she pulled a dusty box off the shelf, *the lack of demon activity is unnerving*. Occasionally short periods of time passed when no evil underworld something was intent on the imminent demise of the Charmed Ones, as she and her two witch sisters were known. However, the lulls were usually followed by a major threat to their mission, existence, or both. The cost of doing business for those who were destined to save the world from supernatural evil over and over again was being in constant jeopardy.

As though to punctuate that point, a plastic tube full of tennis balls on the shelf tipped over. Three rolled out and hit Piper in the head before she could set down the box to freeze them. She couldn't even blame Leo for the harmless indignity. The tennis balls belonged to Phoebe, who had taken up the sport one semester in high school because she wanted an extracurricular athletic activity on her transcript.

Setting the small cardboard box on the bed, Piper rounded up the loose fuzzy balls and dropped them back into the tube. She considered putting it in Cole and Phoebe's closet, but they didn't have any more space for unnecessary stuff than she and Leo did. She set the tube aside and glanced into the box.

"So that's what happened to you!" Piper grinned when she saw a bundle of spiral notebooks stashed with old birthday cards, a valentine Teddy bear, a deflated balloon bouquet, and other souvenirs of events she hadn't thought of in years. The notebooks were stuffed full of recipes she had collected from magazines, newspapers, and TV cooking shows when she was a teenager. She had given them up for lost after searching everywhere in the old Victorian house a couple of years before.

"Everywhere but my closet, apparently," she muttered, "the most obvious place to put them for safekeeping."

As Piper reached for the notebooks, she was

startled by a sudden sound behind her. She whirled, whipping her hands out to freeze. Instead of immobilizing a sneaky demon, she blew up a box of Leo's paperback books.

Piper winced as a blizzard of printed paper, colorful covers, and brown cardboard confetti settled over the clothes still hanging in the closet. A few stray bits drifted into shoes and boots lying on the floor.

When her powers had first emerged, Piper was able to freeze things by slowing down molecules. That ability had eventually expanded to include speeding up molecules, which blasted things apart. After a hazardous adjustment period, she had finally learned to control the destructive power—except in certain extreme circumstances.

Like being more on edge than normal because the demonic world is lying low for reasons that cannot possibly be good, Piper thought.

However, since nothing evil was going down at the moment, she could deal with the immediate calamity of Leo's pulverized books. Although she couldn't remember every title he had accumulated since she had known him, she could replace most of them.

Exhaling with exasperation, Piper left to get a dustpan and broom. At least nobody was home. Paige Matthews, half sister, half-Whitelighter, and the youngest Halliwell witch, was working at South Bay Social Services. Cole Turner, an exdemon and her soon-to-be brother-in-law, was practically living at the university law library lately. With luck, she could remove the evidence of her power gone amok before Leo got back from Yard And Home Discount and Phoebe returned from an interview with Reliable Temps. She so didn't want to explain the embarrassing loss of control.

Phoebe stared across the desk at Donald Ramsey while he studied her application. Roughly thirty with short brown hair, brown eyes, and a classic profile, the interviewer at Reliable Temps was the most attractive human resources interrogator she had met on her months-long job search. However, his above average good looks were the *only* thing that set him apart from the other inflexible people who hadn't hired her.

"I don't have much experience, but I'm a quick learner," Phoebe offered with a smile.

"It took you longer than usual to get your degree, though, didn't it?" Mr. Ramsey didn't look at her as he flipped the application over and moved on to her short résumé.

"Yes, it did." Phoebe decided not to elaborate. Although she had missed a couple of semesters during a typical young-adult rebellious phase, she had also taken a break between leaving New York and returning to San Francisco to learn how to function as a witch. Mr. Ramsey didn't need to know that.

"And you've never been employed in a steady nine-to-five capacity for any length of time." Mr. Ramsey eyed her from under thick, dark eyelashes that were totally wasted on his uptight personality.

"No, but I've worked a variety of jobs when I wasn't attending school," Phoebe pointed out. "Doesn't that make me ideally qualified for temporary positions?"

Mr. Ramsey heaved an unnecessary sigh. "Not if you insist on having flexible hours as your application indicates."

"It wouldn't be all the time," Phoebe said, hiding her displeasure at his contemptuous tone. She wished she could give him razor burn and a receding hairline, but the good witch rules wouldn't allow it, not without consequences she wouldn't like. "Just every now and then."

Phoebe knew that if someone would just give her a chance, she could prove she was efficient and dependable. Then maybe her need for irregular hours wouldn't matter. She had considered lying on her application to get that chance, but she just couldn't be so blatantly dishonest.

"I'm looking for people who will take their assignments seriously." Mr. Ramsey set her application aside and folded his hands. "Our clients expect us to provide employees who will show up on time every day without fail."

"That goes without saying," Phoebe agreed.

"I'm not trying to be difficult, Ms. Halliwell,

but"—Mr. Ramsey leaned forward—"can you honestly say you'll live up to that standard on a job that might last several months?"

No one could promise that, but Phoebe knew her situation involved more than taking an occasional sick or personal day. A Charmed One had to drop everything on a moment's notice when evil threatened an innocent. Working as a temp had seemed like the perfect solution to her unemployment problem. Obviously she had been mistaken.

"No, Mr. Ramsey, I can't." Rising, Phoebe extended her hand. Although the man's superior attitude annoyed her, he was just doing his job. To be fair, she couldn't promise to represent Reliable Temps with one hundred percent reliability. "Thank you for your time."

"You're welcome." Mr. Ramsey stood and shook her hand. "I'll, uh, keep your application on file in case something in your field comes along."

"I'd appreciate that." Phoebe fled the office at a composed walk. She seriously doubted that inexperienced psychology graduates were in much demand as temps. However, it was one more reason to stay current with the latest trends and theories. Since graduating, she had kept up with all the professional psychology journals and popular books so she'd be prepared if a job opportunity did arise.

Stranger things have certainly happened, Phoebe

thought wryly as she slid behind the steering wheel of her car. She turned her cell back on and speed dialed Paige at work. "Hi, Paige. Got a minute?"

"Yeah, but that's all I've got." Paige sounded harried. "The police are on their way here with a hard case juvenile I have to process. How'd the interview go?"

"I bombed as usual," Phoebe said, "but it reminded me of that book you mentioned the other night. The one about relationships in the twenty-first century."

"*Hearts and Heads in Conflict*?" Paige hesitated. "The interview was that tough, huh?"

"Let's just say it reminded me that I'd like to use my psychology degree for something besides hiding a stain on my bedroom wallpaper. Could I stop by to pick up that book?" Phoebe asked adding, "Unless this isn't a good time."

Paige's boss, Mr. Cowan, was incredibly tolerant of his assistant's erratic schedule. The unofficial arrangement made it possible for Paige to work without neglecting her duties as a Charmed One, and Phoebe didn't want to do anything to disrupt it. Since Leo's Whitelighter career was strictly non-profit, Paige and Piper were the only residents of Halliwell Manor that actually made money. Cole was applying to law firms throughout the city, but no one had hired *him*, yet, either.

"It's right here on my desk," Paige said. "I

think I can spare a few seconds to hand it to you."

"Great. I'll be there in twenty minutes or so, depending on traffic." Phoebe hit the end button and put the cell phone in the hands-free device Leo had recently installed on the dash.

As she pulled out of the parking lot, Phoebe considered calling Cole to meet her for lunch. She had to pick up a few psychology books she had ordered through the mall bookstore, but other than that she had nothing pressing to do and nowhere important to be. Lingering over lunch with the love of her life would take the sting out of another botched job interview. However, since Cole would probably accept, she decided not to tempt him.

We'll have plenty of leisurely lunches after Cole joins some prestigious law firm, Phoebe thought as she headed up the freeway ramp. Until then, his time was better spent brushing up on recent case law at the university library than tending to his future wife's bruised ego.

I'll just have to pamper myself with a mocha crème cappuccino at that new cafe in the mall, Phoebe thought with a wistful sigh.

"I've got it right here." Paige held the phone against her shoulder with her chin and flipped open Todd Corman's file. It was identical to the one she had faxed to Ray Marino a few minutes ago.

As Paige scanned Todd's police record again, it wasn't hard to understand why the administrator of Bay Haven wasn't jumping at the chance to take him. The boy had been in trouble with the law since his mother had died five years before. He was only twelve now, but Todd's transgressions ranged from disturbing the peace to destruction of public property to assault on a series of foster parents, none of whom had lasted more than eight months as his court-appointed guardians. If the social services system couldn't get him straightened out, his juvenile rap sheet would be the size of an epic Russian novel when it was sealed in six years.

"This kid obviously goes looking for trouble, Paige," Ray said.

"That's why I called you. I thought Bay Haven was a home for delinquent boys," Paige said with deliberate sarcasm.

Ray sighed. "I've got three other kids here who are finally starting to shape up. This isn't the best time to add a disruptive influence."

Paige shifted her gaze from the file to the sullen boy sitting in Scott's cubicle across the aisle. The freckles spattered across his nose and cheeks did not soften the hard line of a mouth clamped shut. A mop of unruly brown hair desperately needed cutting, but his narrowed brown eyes dared anyone to try. Defiant and hostile, Todd Corman was a perfect example of why she had decided on a career in social services. She wanted to help people, especially those whose circumstances seemed hopeless.

And not just through South Bay, Paige thought. Although it had been difficult to accept having magical powers at first, she had never balked at having to protect the innocent from supernatural bad guys.

Sitting with his arms folded, Todd glared when he caught Paige watching him. He swung his leg so his shoe thudded against the desk, hoping the annoying, repetitive noise would provoke a confrontation.

"That's enough, Todd!" Scott barked and pulled the boy's chair back from his desk.

Paige calmly turned her head and lowered her voice. "Check that file again, Ray. If you don't take him, he'll be sent to C. J."

"County Juvenile?" Ray paused, sighing again. "Then he's really as bad as his file indicates?"

"I don't know," Paige fudged. She couldn't vouch for the boy with any certainty.

The police had found him wandering the downtown streets several hours after John and Lucy Grissom reported that he had run away— again. After the officers dropped Todd off at the clinic, she had tried leaving him in reception with a stack of sports magazines. He had made a break for the door the instant she turned her back. Scott had agreed to keep an eye on him while she tried to work things out with Ray.

"Todd's file says he's an incorrigible," Ray observed. "Nobody thinks he'll ever care enough about anything or anyone to turn his life around—except you."

That's probably true, Paige thought. Todd had been reclassified that morning, which greatly limited her placement options. Even so, she wasn't ready to write him off as a lost cause. Bay Haven, a privately funded institution that dealt specifically with kids who seemed beyond saving, was his best and last hope. For one thing, the home for hard case boys didn't require a mountain of paperwork or a lengthy admissions process. Ray Marino, who was authorized to make an instant decision, just needed some more pointed prodding.

"Don't your patrons expect you to rise to a challenge, Ray?" Paige threw down the gauntlet and crossed her fingers.

Bay Haven relied on the generosity of San Francisco's wealthy to stay operational. If those supporters suspected that the home wasn't providing the promised services, there were other charities they could use as tax deductions.

"Okay, okay!" Ray laughed. "I surrender."

"Is that a yes?" Paige straightened in her chair.

"Affirmative," Ray said. "I need to notify some people and get the transfer process started. Can you keep him there for a few hours and bring him out this afternoon?"

"I'll manage." Paige relaxed. "Thanks, Ray. We'll see you later today."

"I'm looking forward to it," the administrator said.

Paige dropped the phone in its cradle with a sigh of relief. She had never met Ray in person, but he lived at the home and seemed totally devoted to the boys in his care. Despite his initial hesitation, she suspected he enjoyed the challenge of turning die-hard delinquents into solid citizens.

Paige felt relieved as she stepped over to Scott's cubicle to retrieve Todd.

"How'd it go with Bay Haven?" Scott asked with genuine interest.

"Todd's in," Paige announced, smiling. Her good mood dimmed under Todd's malevolent gaze, but she kept her voice neutral. "We'll drive out to Bay Haven this afternoon, Todd. After I process the paper—"

"I'm not going," Todd stated flatly.

Paige wasn't surprised by the boy's ungrateful attitude. He had alienated everyone who had ever tried to help him. According to his psychological profile, he vented his frustrations on whomever or whatever was close by, a compulsion he suddenly chose to demonstrate.

"And you can't make me!" Todd stood up, swept a stack of file folders off Scott's desk, and bolted past Paige.

That's what you think, mister, Paige thought.

Helping those in need might be her calling in life, but Todd Corman was on a fast track to single-handedly wrecking her career and convictions.

Phoebe's reflexes had always been good, but they had been finely honed during her workouts with Cole. When a young boy bolted from a cubicle on a collision course, she reacted without conscious thought or hesitation.

"Whoa there!" Phoebe blocked the escape, grabbing the boy's arms just as Paige arrived and snagged a fistful of t-shirt. Her grip tightened as a vision flooded her mind.

Tendrils of fog swirled around and between two men who faced each other in a darkening twilight. The taller man stood near a high stone wall. His facial features were obscured by shadows, but his black attire was favored by the underworld beings that existed to kill Whitelighters

Darklighter! Phoebe thought, flinching. Her perspective shifted suddenly, revealing the identity of the second man. She gasped as the images abruptly blinked out.

"Not so fast, Todd." Paige spoke sternly to the struggling boy, unaware of her sister's brief precognitive lapse. She glanced at Phoebe with a wry smile. "Great timing, Phoebe. Thanks."

Phoebe just nodded, stunned.

The Darklighter in the vision had been threatening Leo.

Chapter
2

Piper cut a length of shelf paper and placed it in the kitchen cabinet. *Perfect fit*, she thought with a satisfied smile. She had been meaning to reline the shelves for weeks, but until the recent lull, they had been hard pressed just to keep up with cleaning and repairing household demon damage.

Humming along with the hit song that played on the radio, she put stacks of bowls and plates back on the shelf. Usually when she was on edge, domestic puttering and upbeat music calmed her. Today the busywork projects weren't doing the trick.

Piper had finished sweeping up the remains of the paperbacks and emptying the closet a few minutes before Leo returned from the home improvement store. Since her handyman husband didn't need help installing the closet organizer, she had left to make herself useful elsewhere. Now, with the house clean, the laundry done, the kitchen shelves repapered, and no demons to vanquish, she suddenly had free time.

Piper closed the cabinet door and turned off the radio when the song ended. The fast-talking deejay's patter grated like fingernails on a chalkboard, which aggravated her jumpy condition. Being idle didn't alleviate her growing sense of impending doom either.

When in doubt, cook, Piper thought as she unwrapped a half loaf of Italian bread leftover from last night's dinner. After applying a generous coating of garlic butter, Piper put the bread in a shallow pan and into the oven. A quick warm-up would turn the stale bread into a savory side dish for the antipasto she had prepared earlier. As she opened the fridge to check the salad, a loud clanking thump sounded behind her.

Spinning, Piper threw out her hands to freeze.

"It's just me!" Leo exclaimed.

"Leo!" Piper balled her hands into harmless fists and pulled back. Her gaze fell on his tool belt, which was lying on the floor.

"Sorry. It slipped." Leo scooped the tool belt from the floor and dropped it on the table. "You're a little edgy, aren't you? Is something going on that I don't know about?"

Exhaling, Piper shook her head. "No, except

for putting the Piper whammy on various inanimate objects around the house, everything's fine. That's the problem. Nothing awful is happening, and my nerves are shot."

"The scary part is that I understood the logic behind that." Leo pulled out a chair and sat down. "You feel like we're living in the calm before the storm."

"Exactly!" Piper's face brightened. "It's been a week since that weird underworld virus fried the TV, longer since we faced anything lethal."

"With the exception of your quick draw," Leo teased. He snapped his hands out in an exaggerated imitation of Piper's power. "So how many household items have you vanquished today?"

"Rub it in at your peril," Piper shot back as she set the antipasto and a cruet of homemade Italian dressing in front of him. She donned a mitt to retrieve the garlic bread from the oven and gingerly set the hot pan on the stove. "All kidding aside, though . . ."

"What?" Leo prompted. He stuffed a forkful of lettuce and cheese into his mouth and nodded his approval as he chewed.

"I really do have a bad feeling." Piper sliced the bread and dropped the pieces into a basket lined with a cloth napkin. She carried the bread and her smaller antipasto to the table, but she didn't sit down.

Leo reached for a slice of bread. "In general or specifically?"

Taking two mineral waters from the fridge, Piper returned to the table and slumped into a chair. She handed a bottle to Leo. "Like something is just waiting for the right moment to let us have it, and whatever it is . . . it's totally terrible."

"That pretty much describes everything that's ever threatened the Charmed Ones," Leo quipped.

"Which doesn't make anticipation of the next disaster any easier." Piper picked up her fork and poked at her salad.

"I know." Leo's tone turned serious. "But we don't get many chances to just hang around the house doing normal stuff without something fatal breathing down our necks."

"And I just spoiled it by reminding you that any semblance of normality is only temporary." Piper sagged.

"*Everything* is temporary," Leo said. "So let's savor every ordinary minute we can and hope you don't blow up any good guys while we're waiting for the bad guys to strike."

Piper blinked, taken aback for a moment before she realized he was joking.

Leo burst out laughing and ducked when she playfully cuffed his arm.

"Point taken," Piper said, smiling. She knew he was right. It was silly to waste precious demon-free minutes worrying about the next, inevitable attack. "So how long before you're done installing the closet organizer?"

"Another hour or so." Leo helped himself to more bread then cocked his head. "Why?"

"Well, I thought I might get started on my high-yield garden this afternoon." Piper lifted a notebook off the hutch and placed it on the table.

Leo munched salad as he studied the grids Piper had marked off and labeled on the rectangular diagram. "Do you really expect all these different vegetables to grow in such a small area?"

"Yes, that's why this is called a high-yield garden," Piper explained. "It's scientifically designed for a variety of vegetables and herbs in a limited space. I found an article about it in an old magazine Grams had stashed in the attic."

Leo nodded. "Well, you do need a lot of herbs for talismans and potions."

"Not to mention casseroles," Piper added. "What I need *now* is help digging up the backyard."

Leo looked skeptical. "Are Phoebe and Paige all right with that?"

"I finally convinced them," Piper admitted.

Half of the small backyard was planted with ornamental flowers and shrubs. The remaining grassy area was barely big enough for lawn chairs and a table. None of the Halliwell witches spent much time outside soaking up the sun, but it was nice to know they could if they wanted to. However, growing food *and* spell ingredients appealed to their basic witch instincts.

"Then just show me where to shovel." As Leo reached for a third piece of garlic bread, he caught Piper's pointed gaze. "I can't let this go to waste."

"Uh-huh." Piper arched an eyebrow. Leo didn't have an ounce of fat on his lean body, but she couldn't resist the opportunity to zing him back for his comment about her quick draw. "Maybe we'd better dig a bigger garden so that bread doesn't go to *your* waist."

Leo froze with his hand poised over the breadbasket. "Am I gaining weight?"

"Are you sure you saw Leo, Phoebe?" Paige asked with a quick glance at Todd. After Phoebe had interrupted his attempted escape, she had taken him into her cubicle and ordered him to sit. Now she and Phoebe huddled by Scott's cubicle. Scott had gone to the copy room, and they whispered so Todd couldn't overhear. A report on Phoebe's vision couldn't wait, but she didn't dare let him out of her sight.

Especially now that I know he's somehow connected with a Darklighter that's a threat to Leo, Paige thought with a shiver.

"I'm sure." Phoebe looked as grim as Paige felt. "At least Leo hadn't been attacked . . . yet."

"That's something, I guess." Paige rubbed her arms to relieve a psychological chill. "How does Todd fit in?"

"I don't know." Phoebe shrugged with a glance at the boy.

Paige followed her sister's worried gaze. Todd sat staring at the floor as though he could care less what the two women were talking about.

"Why is he here at South Bay, Paige?" Phoebe turned away from Todd as she spoke.

"He's an orphan and a habitual runaway with a rap sheet way too long for his age," Paige explained.

"Then I guess there's not much chance he's a future Whitelighter," Phoebe stated.

That idea was so absurd, Paige would have laughed if the circumstances depicted in her sister's vision weren't so dire.

Darklighters carried crossbows armed with poisoned arrows that were fatal to Leo's kind. They hunted Whitelighters and those truly self-less individuals who would become Whitelighters after they died. Given Todd's turbulent history, it was safe to assume that he wasn't a candidate for guardian angel status.

"One in a million maybe," Paige said. "Right now, Ray Marino over at Bay Haven and I are probably the only thing standing between Todd and a life of crime."

Phoebe's brow furrowed in puzzled thought.

"What?" Paige prompted.

"If Todd isn't Whitelighter material," Phoebe said softly, "Leo won't be protecting him from the Darklighter. So he must be protecting Todd from something else."

"And the Darklighter just happens to pick that moment to go after Leo?" Paige frowned. "That sounds a little too convenient."

"Maybe." Phoebe sighed. "I suppose Todd could be an accidental witness with no connection to whatever brings Leo to the scene."

Like a Darklighter who wants to add a couple of notches to his crossbow? Paige wondered.

"But Todd caused the vision," Phoebe continued, voicing her train of thought. "Whether he's directly involved or not, he'll be present when the Darklighter challenges Leo."

"What if *I'm* the target?" Paige asked. She was a half-Whitelighter, which qualified her for the Darklighter hit list, and she would be spending a lot of time with Todd while he adjusted to living at Bay Haven. "Maybe Leo is there to protect *me*? That is his job."

"That's possible, I guess," Phoebe said, "but I didn't see you."

That doesn't mean I won't *be there*, Paige thought, but she didn't point that out. Being in danger, even from a dreaded Darklighter, wouldn't override her professional or Charmed obligation regarding Todd.

"Is Todd in danger?" Paige asked. Bystanders were sometimes caught in the crossfire between the forces of good and evil.

"I don't think so, but I can't be sure."

Phoebe's eyes narrowed as she studied Todd again. "I saw things through his eyes, but it was almost as though—"

"He didn't care what was going on?" Paige finished.

With his dirty sneakers, faded jeans, and unkempt hair, the boy looked like any kid in trouble, forlorn and vulnerable. Then he looked up, reminding Paige that her efforts on his behalf might be in vain. His unflinching gaze was devoid of any feeling—for himself or anyone else.

Phoebe drew Paige farther from the cubicle. "Since we don't know what events lead up to Leo's run-in with the Darklighter, we should probably keep an eye on the kid."

"Yeah, I agree," Paige said, "but I'm supposed to drive him out to Bay Haven this afternoon. It's a private home for hard case boys."

Since Todd was a delinquent and completely entrenched in the child welfare system, Paige didn't see any way to avoid that. He was too untrustworthy to take to Halliwell Manor, and the County Juvenile Detention Center was the only other alternative. To facilitate the settling in process, county regulations limited visitations, even with a caseworker. The over crowded conditions at the government center would make it too risky and difficult to orb in undetected, which she would have to do. With Leo's safety at stake, some clandestine surveillance would be required.

"How secure is Bay Haven?" Phoebe asked.

"Probably as tight as any minimum security facility." Paige tried to remember the statistics listed in the county records about the private home.

Before the property had been bequeathed to the charitable foundation that managed it, Bay Haven was the estate of a prominent, old money family. Surrounded by forest in an isolated area outside the city, the mansion was not escape proof, but a runaway wouldn't get very far on foot.

"It's in a remote location with qualified staff in residence," Paige said. "He might be safer there than anywhere else. It'll definitely be easier for me to stay in touch with him there than at County. I can always orb in to orb him out if necessary too."

"And so can Leo," Phoebe said. "Just as long as it's during the light of day or the dark of night."

"Day or night?" Paige had no idea what her sister meant. "What else is there?"

"Fog at dusk." Phoebe looked her in the eye. "The exact conditions I saw in my vision."

Phoebe kept both hands on the steering wheel while she talked to Piper on her cell. The new hands-free device worked perfectly.

"Let me get this straight," Piper said. "Some unknown Darklighter is coming after Leo but we don't know when or where."

Routed through the radio speakers, Piper's voice sounded clear and full. *And totally stressed, understandably,* Phoebe thought.

"That's about the size of it," Phoebe said. "But since Leo isn't with Todd Corman, he's not in any immediate danger. Besides, whatever's going to happen doesn't happen in broad daylight."

"Well, that might help," Piper said. "After Leo finishes the closet organizer and digs up the yard, he'll be too tired to leave the house tonight—unless it's a Whitelighter emergency."

Which is probably how the Darklighter intends to lure him, Phoebe thought with a sigh. Like Paige, Leo wouldn't neglect his duty to protect himself when an innocent was in trouble.

"Why is he digging up the yard?" Phoebe asked, changing the subject.

"I'm planting a vegetable-and-herb garden, remember?" Piper explained.

"Oh, right." Phoebe had forgotten that Piper's latest domestic hobby involved sacrificing a large portion of the small backyard lawn. Piper had been so enthusiastic about the urban mini-farm, she and Paige hadn't had the heart to veto the project.

"Look," Phoebe went on, "I was going to stop by the mall to pick up some magazines I ordered, but maybe I should come straight home." She glanced at the copy of *Hearts and Heads in Conflict* lying on the seat. Reading

Paige's paperback would help her cope with the impending Darklighter strike and being jobless for a couple of days.

"How'd the job interview go?" Piper asked, as though reading Phoebe's mind.

"I don't think the phone will be ringing off the hook with temporary employment offers," Phoebe said.

"Then go get your magazines," Piper ordered. Her crisp tone suggested it wouldn't be wise to argue. "We can't do anything about the Darklighter until we have more information, so, unless there's an unscheduled eclipse that blots out the sun this afternoon, another hour won't matter. I'll call your cell if anything happens before you get back."

After signing off, Phoebe felt as though someone had thrown a wet blanket over her life. Although she could usually find the silver lining in the darkest cloud, her optimistic nature wasn't rising to the occasion this time. Ordinarily she didn't lament the lack of normality in her magical existence. Today, however, everything seemed to remind her that the ordinary daily routine Piper longed for was probably an impossible dream for all the Charmed Ones.

"Maybe that mocha crème cappuccino will lift my spirits," Phoebe mumbled as she parked and turned off the ignition. She stepped outside, locked the car, and turned toward the mall entrance with the nagging feeling that the brief respite from marauding demons was about to end—perhaps tragically.

In a parking space just ahead, a young woman held a toddler by one hand as she struggled to put a folding stroller into the trunk of her car. When the child picked up a candy wrapper from the pavement, the woman yanked it out of his hand and tossed it aside.

"Don't put that in your mouth, Karl!" The woman snapped. "Dirty! Yuck!"

The little boy began to bawl.

"Please, stop crying." The frazzled mom lifted the sobbing boy and buckled him into his car seat. "We'll go to Turkey Tots for ice cream right after my dentist appointment."

"I wan' candy." Karl sniffled and wiped his nose with his hand.

"Whatever." The woman looked at her watch as she slid into the driver's seat. "I hope they haven't canceled me because we're late. If Kangaroo Playpen doesn't have a day care opening for you soon, I'm going to go nuts!"

As she watched them drive away, Phoebe was struck by the fact that the woman and child lived in a completely different world. She couldn't remember what life had been like when missing a dentist appointment was a catastrophe, and she could only imagine how critical quality day care could be to a parent's sanity.

Is she going to hold Karl on her lap while she has her teeth cleaned? Phoebe wondered as she entered the mall and turned toward Carousel Books. Fighting off a lower level demon that spat fire or oozed acid seemed easier by comparison.

Dentists and kids were forgotten as Phoebe gave the bookstore clerk her name. When the girl left to get her order from the back room, she browsed through the bargain books. A man in a business suit caught her eye as he paid another clerk for a daily financial newspaper.

Tucking the paper under his arm, the man left with a cell phone glued to his ear. Tall, slim, and impeccably dressed, he reminded Phoebe of Cole when Cole had worked for the district attorney's office, before his demon identity had been revealed. Now Belthazor was dead and Cole was just a regular guy.

Unemployed with an evil past, but one hundred percent human, Phoebe thought. At least she didn't have to hide her magical identity from Cole. Since total trust was vital to a successful marriage, that was a plus.

"Here they are." The clerk slipped Phoebe's journals into a plastic bag imprinted with the store's logo. "That'll be thirty-five seventy-six."

Phoebe sighed as she handed the girl her credit card. Piper knew that she needed the periodicals to stay current in her field. Still, she hoped she or Cole would find work before she had to ask for money to pay the bill.

As Phoebe turned to leave, the clerk answered the phone.

"Are you sure you're too sick to come in, Bethany?" The clerk paused. "No, I don't mind taking your shift. I'm over the limit on my credit card this month so I can use the extra cash."

As she headed toward the food court, Phoebe was again struck by the differences in her reality and the clerk's. They both had money troubles, but the other girl didn't have to worry about defending her brother-in-law from a supernatural bad guy with a lethal crossbow in addition to paying down her credit card.

That's like twisting the knife, Phoebe realized. She and her sisters weren't exempt from the ordinary problems that most people had to deal with, but most people weren't responsible for the fate of the world, too.

After ordering a mocha crème cappuccino to go from a vender that specialized in exotic coffees and cakes, Phoebe sat at a nearby table to wait. The depression she had first felt when she knew that Donald Ramsey wasn't going to hire her continued to intensify. Although she really wanted a job that utilized her knowledge of psychology, she was ready to settle for anything, except maybe slinging burgers for minimum wage. Ever since she had agreed to marry Cole, she had been tormented by the idea that she'd never accomplish anything beyond being a wife and a witch.

Not that being a wife and a witch is bad, she thought. Piper thrived on being married, and although her older sister sometimes said she resented the dangerous downside of being a powerful witch, she was good at magic, too. But Piper's achievements didn't stop there. Although Phoebe and Prue had mortgaged the Manor to finance P3, credit for the concept, management, and ultimate success of the club belonged entirely to Piper.

Paige wasn't a slouch either. Although she was single and liked it, Phoebe's half sister was a shining example of Halliwell heart and resilience. Paige had quickly adapted to her magical powers and the inherent perils of being a Charmed One. Totally dedicated to saving innocents from supernatural evil, she had also made a career of helping those who were threatened by mortal villains and circumstances.

And just like Piper, Paige never turns her back on duty, Phoebe reflected. *Not even when it involves a boy like Todd Corman, who either doesn't know the difference between right and wrong or simply doesn't care.*

Phoebe couldn't say the same about herself. More often than not lately, she felt as though she was taking much more than she was giving—except for the visions.

"Your order's ready, miss." The man behind the coffee counter pressed a plastic top onto her cup.

"Thanks." Suddenly anxious to get home, Phoebe paid the man, took her coffee, and left.

Phoebe rushed back to her car wishing her vision of the Darklighter had been more detailed. Her glimpses of the future and occasional flashes of the past had made the difference between success and failure or life and death for the innocents she and her sisters helped too often.

This time, though, a young boy's life was somehow entwined with an evil entity that threatened Leo's very existence.

Chapter

3

"Are you sure you don't want anything, Todd?" Paige asked as she exited the freeway.

Two mini-mart gas stations, a fast-food restaurant, and one motel occupied the intersection formed by the interstate and a two-lane state highway. Until Lucy Grissom sent his belongings, Todd had nothing but the clothes he was wearing. Although Bay Haven would provide the basics, Paige had offered to buy him a few essential personal items, such as a toothbrush and comb.

"Are your ears stuffed up?" Todd Corman's brown eyes blazed as he snapped his head around. "I said no the last time you asked me."

Several cutting retorts flashed through Paige's mind, but she resisted the urge to snap back. Words that weren't backed up by action would have no effect on the belligerent boy.

Except to unleash another barrage of insults, Paige thought as she braked at the stop sign.

"Just leave me alone, okay?" Todd rolled his eyes and folded his arms.

"Don't think so." Paige turned right onto the highway, then right again into a gas station. She stopped the green VW at the edge of parking lot, away from the store and the pumps.

She had put up with Todd's hostility and verbal abuse during the forty-five minute ride, hoping to breach his defenses with patience and understanding. She hadn't even scratched his emotional armor, but he had managed to dent her professional pride.

Most of the displaced kids Paige met were desperate for security and drawn to anyone who honestly cared. Any remnants of trust or need Todd Corman felt had been shattered beyond repair or buried too deep to reach. At the moment, his uncooperative attitude and antagonistic tongue were his worst enemies. If Todd didn't learn some respect in a hurry, Ray Marino would kick him out of Bay Haven before she cleared the driveway on her way home.

"There're a few things you need to know before we get to Bay Haven, Todd."

"Forget it." Todd reached to punch his seatbelt release. "I'm out of here, lady."

"You're not going anywhere," Paige said, resting her arm on the top of Todd's seat. Both doors were locked.

"Just try to stop me," Todd muttered as he reached to punch the seatbelt release.

Paige pointed toward the depressed plastic lock tab in the passenger door. "Lock."

"You're kidding, right?" Todd was looking at the seatbelt fastener and didn't notice the small orb stream. The lock button moved from the door into Paige's hand.

"My sense of humor bailed sixty seconds after we left the office." Paige closed her fist around the button and sat back as the orb particles dispersed. Without the plastic piece, the mechanism couldn't be unlocked.

"I'm not laughing either." Todd slipped off the seatbelt and turned to tug on the door handle.

Paige hid a smile when the door didn't open.

Cursing under his breath, Todd jerked the handle several times. Then he reached for the lock tab. When he realized it was missing, he pounded the padded door with his fist.

"Throwing a tantrum won't help," Paige said calmly, "but you might take a hint. You're just as stuck in the child welfare system as you are in this car. Fits and fighting won't do anything but make things worse."

"Maybe," Todd sneered, "but it'll make *me* feel better."

"Not for long." Paige leaned back, holding his gaze, her expression impassive. "You've only got two choices right now, Todd. Clean up your act so you can stay at Bay Haven, or bottom out at County Juvenile."

"Some choice," Todd scoffed, averting his gaze. "Why should I care?"

"Good behavior is rewarded at Bay Haven, even if you're just faking it to get by," Paige said. "If you give a little, the staff will give back."

"Give me a hard time, probably," Todd said.

"That's up to you." Normally Paige wouldn't be so candid with someone so young, but nothing less than the brutal truth would impress the stubborn adolescent. "If you can't cut it at Bay Haven, you'll be another loser at County Juvenile, doing nothing and going nowhere until they turn you loose when you're eighteen."

"Doesn't matter to me." Todd set his mouth and stared at the dashboard. "They're both jails."

"Personally, I'd rather have my own room on a country estate than a bunk and a locker at County." Paige put the car in gear. "Buckle up."

Todd snapped his seatbelt into the buckle without looking at her.

At least he didn't argue, Paige thought as she pocketed the plastic lock tab and pulled back onto the highway. All things considered, that was a major victory. Maybe he had gotten the message.

Paige didn't intrude on Todd's thoughts as she drove through the California countryside. This was her first trip to Bay Haven too, and she

was intensely curious about the home and its
new administrator.

The Carrington Foundation had established
Bay Haven as a last resort home for delinquent
boys in the early 1970s. The facility also served
as a certified school with a full-time teacher and
volunteer tutors. The home had thrived on the
estate trust fund and donations for twenty-five
years. The death of the home's elderly trustee
and several years of financial mismanagement
had almost forced the home to close. Then the
Carrington Foundation board had hired Ray
Marino.

In less than a year, Ray's innovative fund raising skills and cost cutting tactics had put the
institution back on solid financial footing. He
had also earned the respect of social services
professionals. According to the grapevine, Ray
had a soft heart, but he practiced tough love and
ran the home like a benevolent dictator.

A flash of brown caught Paige's eye. She
pointed out at windshield. "There's a deer!"

Todd looked up as the animal darted into the
woods. He shrugged, as though that would
negate the spark of interest. "Big deal."

Paige let him have the last word. Having lost
her adoptive parents in a car accident when she
was a teenager, she understood the need to lash
out. She had weathered three of the emotional
phases people usually experienced in the after-
math of tragedy: denial, anger, and acceptance.

Todd hadn't gotten past anger, but with help and encouragement, she believed he would move on and turn his life around.

If he survives the foggy future Phoebe saw in her vision, Paige reminded herself. Aside from Todd's disagreeable attitude and complaints, the only blot on the balmy afternoon was his undetermined role in the events that would bring Leo and a Darklighter face to face.

Paige shuddered, wondering if she had a part to play in the Darklighter scenario too. Her gloomy musings ended when the car rounded a curve and Bay Haven came into view.

"I think you've got the wrong address." The sight of the mansion apparently took Todd by surprise. His mouth fell open in astonishment, but Paige pretended she hadn't noticed.

"No, this is it," Paige said as she drove between the decorative stone pillars that flanked the entrance.

A large iron gate stood open. Flowers and trimmed shrubbery grew in landscaped beds in front of a high stone wall designed to keep intruders out. An oversized mailbox had been built into a free-standing stone pillar on the roadway.

The stone mansion sat on a rolling expanse of green meadow surrounded by forest. Large oaks and other shade trees dotted the manicured lawn and lined the long, curved driveway. A monument to the elegance of life in the early

twentieth century, the stately house still evoked
a sense of tranquil grandeur and awe.

"This looks like some rich guy's place." Todd
scowled. "They probably keep the kids in the
basement so we don't mess up anything."

"Dorm rooms are on the third floor, classrooms on the second." Paige stopped in front of
the house and turned off the engine. "Let's go."

Todd eyed her with exasperation. "My door
lock's broken, remember?"

"So climb out my side," Paige said matter-of-
factly, making a mental note to replace the tab on
her way back to town. She motioned Todd to
lead the way up several stone steps to the front
portico.

A trim but fit man wearing casual slacks and
an open neck, short-sleeved shirt opened the
door. "Paige Matthews and Todd, I presume."

"Right on both counts." Paige smiled and
shook the man's extended hand.

"Ray Marino." In his mid-thirties with a no-
nonsense, take-charge demeanor, Ray was
attractive in a lean, rugged way. A short, military
style haircut complimented his square jaw, thick
dark eyebrows, and brooding brown eyes.

"Come on in." Ray stepped back, holding the
door open.

Paige entered the large foyer behind Todd,
taking in the interior with a glance. The double
doors on the right led into a library. Through the
windows in the French doors on the left, she

could see into the large drawing room. The worn but tasteful furniture and lack of entertainment electronics indicated that the room was used for business and adult social gatherings. The boys had a community TV room upstairs.

A staircase curved upward to a wide landing and more stairs that were hidden from view. Two straight backed chairs and a long library table stood against the far foyer wall. She guessed that the hallway to the right of the furniture led to the kitchen and dining area at the back of the house.

"Why don't you wait out here a few minutes, Todd," Ray said, placing his hand on the boy's shoulder.

Todd flinched, but recovered quickly. "Aren't you afraid that I'll run away?"

"No." Ray glanced up at a surveillance camera and waved Paige toward the library, which served as an office. "There're just a couple things we need to go over, Paige."

"Of course." Paige saw Todd watching her from the corner of her eye. For a moment, she thought he looked slightly panicked. However, when she turned to meet his gaze, he looked away with a huff of disdain.

Paige sighed, hoping she wouldn't regret pressing Ray to take Todd into Bay Haven.

As she walked by the administrator, Paige noted the placement of two more cameras on the landing and the back of the foyer. Two others hung in opposite corners of the extensive library, leaving no doubt that the whole house was wired to spy. Cabinets built into the interior wall held a bank of monitors. Given the boys' histories as runaways, she couldn't fault the need to watch over them.

"Please, sit down." Ray wasted no time with amenities. He was seated with Todd's file open by the time Paige settled into the comfortable chair opposite him.

Paige shifted position, hoping her survey of the room wasn't too obvious. Since she or Leo might have to orb in to check on Todd, she had to know as much about the layout as possible. The door in the end wall was closed, but the door on her right opened into another, smaller office.

"I want to be certain I understand Todd's whole story," Ray explained. "The kids we take in aren't usually anxious to talk about themselves, and half the time what they do say is hogwash. But then, you know that."

"Sadly, yes." Paige nodded.

Ray leafed through the pages she had faxed him earlier. "According to this, his mother died of a bacterial infection five years ago."

"When Todd was seven," Paige confirmed. "Kari worked a minimum wage job so money was tight. She waited too long to check into an emergency room, and they couldn't save her."

"What a waste." Ray's sigh reflected the

despair Paige so often felt because she couldn't help everyone who needed it. "He doesn't have any other family?"

"Not that the authorities have been able to find," Paige said.

"What happened to the father?" Ray asked.

"Unknown." Paige elaborated in anticipation of Ray's next question. "There's no official record, nothing on Todd's birth certificate or anything, but Kari told Todd that his dad's name was Brian Jamieson. He worked construction and left before Todd was born."

"A rat fleeing the sinking ship," Ray muttered.

"Maybe, but it's also possible he didn't know Kari was pregnant." Paige had learned not to assume anything. Shortly after becoming a Charmed One, she had assumed a father was abusing a child. Contrary to the initial evidence, the mother was guilty. That was a mistake she would not repeat.

Nodding, Ray turned over the paper and scanned the next page. "This boy runs through foster parents faster than boiling water melts ice."

"That's why I called you," Paige said. "John and Lucy Grissom hung in with Todd for eight months of almost constant heartache and disruption."

Ray glanced at the file. "This says Todd broke almost every window in the Grissom's house before he took off."

"And the living room TV," Paige said. "Because they wouldn't let him watch an R-rated horror movie. I certainly don't blame them for calling it quits. Most people's tolerance would have reached the breaking point long before now."

"What makes you think he's worth any more effort?" Ray asked bluntly, looking Paige in the eye.

"Nothing but a hunch." Paige sighed. "And my own stubborn refusal to give up without a fight."

Ray hesitated then nodded, smiling. "That's all I need to know."

Todd sat in one of the uncomfortable chairs and let out a long sigh, fighting back a rush of emotion. His mother was gone, and nothing would bring her back. It was foolish to think Paige Matthews was anything like her just because they looked alike.

Sort of, Todd thought with a pang of sadness. Paige was tall with dark hair and brown eyes like his mom, but that was all. He was pretty sure his mother had never worn bright red lipstick. The few photos he had of Kari Corman were fading, and it got harder to remember the details of her face as time passed. He remembered other things, though.

She had smiled a lot, sometimes even when she was trying to be stern, and she had always listened when he talked. Although he hadn't ever done anything really wrong back then, he never got away with anything. He had been in time-out a lot, but his mom always forgave him, and she didn't stay angry. For some weird reason, Paige had reminded him of how much he missed her.

But they're not really alike, Todd insisted to himself. *My mom wouldn't leave me in some fancy home for boys out in the middle of nowhere just because I broke a few windows.*

Todd's eyes narrowed as he recalled the last time he had seen Lucy and John Grissom, right before he heaved a baseball through the TV screen.

"If you throw that ball, Todd," Lucy had said, *"you're going back to social services tonight. I can't take any more."*

"We won't *take any more,"* John had added.

Todd had thrown the ball, smashing the TV before he ran out of the house. Eluding capture, he had hurled rocks through several windows before he had vanished into the night.

His real mother wouldn't have let him watch that horror movie either, and she would have been furious when he had a screaming tantrum. But she wouldn't have threatened to abandon him the way Lucy had.

And now Paige, Todd thought. She seemed nice, but Lucy had been nice too at first. Then, like all his foster parents, she had stopped caring the instant he messed up. He wasn't going to trust anyone ever again, not even a social worker that seemed nice and sort of looked like his mom.

The sound of a cat mewing snagged Todd's attention. Annoyed for feeling sorry for himself, he watched a yellow tabby slink along the base of the wall. It was thin with coarse fur and a furtive manner. When he shifted position, it stopped dead to stare at him with yellow eyes.

"What's the matter, cat? Having a bad day?" Todd slowly leaned over, extending his hand. "Me too."

A high-pitched animal screech followed by a shriek of human pain and a loud crash cut Ray off.

"What was that?" Paige sprang out of her chair.

"The cat." Ray bolted into the foyer. "What's going on out here?"

Paige stopped in the doorway just as a yellow tabby cat raced up the stairs. One of the chairs was lying on its side by the library table. Todd stood by the table with his hand clamped over his arm.

"That stupid cat scratched me for no reason!" Todd yelled. His face was red with outrage.

"I doubt that," Ray said. "Hadie wouldn't attack except to defend herself."

"I just wanted to pet her." Todd glared at Ray.

Paige frowned. Todd's insistence was persuasive, if only because he didn't usually care if he was caught doing something wrong. He flaunted his transgressions like a badge of defiance. If some other boy had tormented the cat in the past, Hadie might have clawed Todd in anticipation of being hurt.

"How bad is the scratch?" Paige asked.

"I'll live." Todd jerked his arm back when Ray tried to examine the injury.

"Fine." Ray held his hands palm up and stepped back. "I'll show you where we keep the first-aid supplies when I give you the basic new-kid tour. You can take what you need to your room."

"Whatever." Todd's shoulders sagged slightly.

As though he's resigned to some horrible fate, Paige thought.

"He's probably hungry," Paige said. "Except for a doughnut one of the police officers gave him this morning, he hasn't eaten since last night."

"I think Chuck will bend the rules for an emergency sandwich," Ray said with a half-smile. "Just this once."

The administrator's lame attempt at humor fell flat, Paige noticed. Todd had completely closed himself off again. She knew there was nothing she could say that would make the boy feel better about anything, but she didn't want

him to feel completely abandoned, either. She
reached into her bag and pulled out a business
card and a pen.

"Here's my card in case you need anything."
Paige wrote her home telephone number on the
back.

"I won't need anything from you," Todd
sneered.

"You never know." Paige held out the card.
"Take it."

Rolling his eyes, Todd took the card. He
stared at it for a moment then suddenly shoved
it back into Paige's hand. "Go away."

"I'll be in touch." Addressing Ray, Paige
slipped the business card into her pocket and
caught Todd's gaze for a brief moment. He deliberately turned his back, and she left without saying good-bye. The only way to convince him she
was not walking out of his life was to be there for
him in the days, weeks, and months ahead.

Piper sat on her heels and pushed her hair back
with a gloved hand. Leo worked ahead of her,
using a pointed spade to overturn the lawn. She
had followed behind with a handheld three-
pronged garden rake, breaking the large dirt
clumps into smaller pieces and separating out
the grass.

"I'm ready for a break." Piper dropped the
small tool and brushed dirt off her knees as she
stood up. "How about you?"

Leo drove the spade into the ground and rested his arms on the handle. "I'll keep going. We're not even half done yet."

"Yeah, mutilating a yard isn't as easy as it looks." Piper studied their progress as she pulled off her gloves. They had tied red ribbons to the sprinkler heads so they wouldn't accidentally puncture the plastic underground pipes. Next they had stretched string between wooden stakes at the four corners to mark off the small garden plot. However, plowing the six-by-ten-foot area with a shovel was turning out to be a lot more work than either of them had anticipated.

"Do you want something to drink?" Piper asked.

"A gallon of ice-cold water sounds good," Leo quipped.

"Coming right up." Piper sighed with relief when she entered the cool interior of the house. She paused by the sink to wipe the grime off her face with a damp towel before she opened the pantry. If two hours of hard labor had given her an appetite, Leo had to be hungry too.

Basic cheese and crackers with Leo's favorite hot mustard sounds good, Piper thought as she pulled a box of whole-wheat wafers off the shelf. She shrieked, dropped the box, and froze a startled, furry intruder.

"What is it?" Phoebe raced in from the living room clutching a paperback book. Her finger was tucked between the pages to mark her place. "Don't tell me we have a demon in the pantry."

"We don't have a demon in the pantry." Piper stepped aside. "We've got a mouse."

"A frozen mouse." Phoebe stared at the tiny, unmoving creature on the shelf. It sat on its haunches with eyes wide and ears flattened. "He looks more terrified than terrifying."

"It surprised me," Piper huffed. She knew she had overreacted to the rodent lurking behind the wheat crackers, but that was partly because Phoebe's vision had aggravated her frayed nerves. Waiting for some underworld evil to strike was unsettling, but not as disturbing as the threat against Leo. A Darklighter's poison was the only substance in the universe that could kill a Whitelighter—for good.

"Freezing him was a little drastic, wasn't it?" Phoebe asked.

"Not as drastic as blowing him up," Piper observed. In addition to the regrettable loss of life, an exploded mouse would have created a disgusting mess.

"True." Phoebe shuddered. "We can't just let him go, though. One little mouse can munch through our stash of snack crackers in no time."

"Not to mention giving us the creeps every time we want something from the pantry." Piper picked up the crackers and set the box on the counter. Then she opened a cabinet, held up a large coffee can, and popped the plastic lid. "So we'll trap him while he's frozen and set him free—outside."

"That works," Phoebe said. "Need any help?"

"You're kidding, right?" Piper looked at her sister askance. "It's a mouse, not some unspeakable supernatural horror."

"A mouse that you freaked out and froze," Phoebe reminded her, hastening to add, "but considering I saw Leo squaring off with a Darklighter, you're allowed a freebie freak out."

"You're vision isn't the only problem," Piper admitted. "It's been so long since the last demon attack, I'm a nervous wreck. I know this sounds weird, but I'll be glad when something horrendous finally happens. Then maybe I'll relax."

"Catch the mouse, Piper. I'm going to take advantage of the no-demon zone." Phoebe waved the book as she headed back to the living room.

The freeze wore off the frightened mouse just as Piper approached the shelf. She immobilized it with another quick zap, trapped it in the coffee can, and gave the can to Leo.

Leo lifted the edge of the plastic lid and frowned. "It's frozen."

"I know. End of discussion." Piper smiled tightly and spoke over her shoulder as she headed back into the house. "Snacks and drinks will be ready in a minute."

The phone rang as the screen door banged closed behind her.

"Hello." Piper tucked the phone under her chin as she opened the refrigerator.

Phoebe picked up the living room cordless a second later. "Halliwell residence."

"It's Paige. I'm glad I've got both of you so I'll only have to go through this once." Paige sounded stressed.

"Hang on while I put you on the speaker-phone." Piper set a hunk of cheddar cheese on the counter and elbowed the fridge door closed. She punched the speakerphone button and replaced the receiver.

Phoebe hung up and returned to the kitchen. She grabbed the wheat crackers on her way by the counter and carried the box to the table. "Okay, Paige. What's up?"

"I just dropped Todd off at Bay Haven," Paige said. "Something doesn't feel right."

Piper paused with the knife raised over the cheese. "Because he triggered Phoebe's vision or something else?"

"Something involving the Darklighter?" Phoebe asked going directly to the point.

"I don't know." Paige sighed. "I just can't shake the feeling that this kid is in bigger trouble than I thought."

Piper sliced cheese as she listened to Paige recount Todd's introduction to the private home. Just as her jumpy nerves had gotten the better of her that day, she suspected Paige's concern about the boy was more acute because of the vision. That wasn't surprising, but she didn't understand why the incident with the cat was so important.

"Maybe Todd *did* pull the cat's tail or something, Paige," Piper said.

"Then why would he be so upset?" Paige seemed genuinely perplexed. "He didn't react at all when we confronted him about breaking the Grissom's windows or running away, but he was incensed when Ray insinuated that he had harmed the cat."

"He may have a definitive sense of justice," Phoebe suggested. "Distorted, perhaps, but defined."

"What do you mean?" Paige asked.

"I'm just guessing," Phoebe cautioned, "based on what you've told us about this boy, Paige."

"I understand," Paige said. "So guess."

Piper set the plate of sliced cheddar on the table with three jars of mustard: hot, spicy, and her favorite, sweet-hot. Phoebe had her complete attention as she poured ice and lemonade into three glasses.

"Chances are Todd expects to get caught and punished for the things he deliberately does wrong," Phoebe said. "He accepts that because he's guilty, but he can't tolerate being blamed for something he didn't do."

When Paige hesitated, Piper could visualize her younger sister chewing her lip as she mulled over the new information.

"Then my instincts were correct," Paige said after a long moment, "and Todd didn't hurt the cat."

"Probably not," Phoebe agreed.

"What's the significance of that?" Piper handed Phoebe a glass of lemonade and set the other glasses on the table. Leo had worked hard all day, and he needed a sit-down cheese-and-cracker break whether he wanted one or not. She opened the screen door to call him inside.

Paige's sigh was audible through the speakers. "Maybe nothing, but it's better than if he had deliberately tormented a defenseless animal."

"Don't take too much comfort in that, Paige," Phoebe said. "Some of history's worst tyrants loved animals."

Piper caught Leo's eye and waved him to come in. She waited until he jammed the spade into the ground and started toward the house before she went back inside and sat down.

"Point taken," Paige conceded, "but I'd still feel better if Leo could pop in and check up on him."

Piper turned toward the phone. "You want Leo to orb into Bay Haven? Now?"

"It's a long time before dusk," Paige said, referring to the time of day in Phoebe's vision.

"Is that boy in trouble already?" Leo went straight to the sink to wash his hands.

"That's what I want you to find out, Leo," Paige said.

"What are you going to be doing, Paige?" Piper asked. A hint of unintended accusation infected her tone.

"Working." The sharp edge in Paige's retort softened when she added, "I want to start a search for Todd's father right away. Maybe I'll turn up something about Brian Jamieson the other agencies missed. It's worth a shot, anyway."

Piper shifted uneasily. They weren't sure what Todd's role was in the good-versus-evil equation with the Darklighter.

"Since Leo can re-form in invisible mode," Paige went on, "he can watch without being seen."

"Yes, I can." Leo stopped by the table and picked up a glass. He downed half the lemonade then topped a cracker with cheese and mustard.

Piper just nodded. Until they proved otherwise, Todd Corman was an innocent under their protection. Leo had to go regardless of the danger to himself.

"I just pulled into the clinic parking lot," Paige said. "Can you meet me here, Leo? There're some things you should know about the layout at Bay Haven."

"Be right there." Leo finished off the lemonade.

"Thanks." Paige's cell disconnected.

Phoebe sensed Piper's misgivings and tried to reassure her. "My visions are usually accurate,

Piper. There's no fog and the sun won't set for hours, so Leo should be perfectly safe on an invisible surveillance."

"I know you're probably right, Phoebe," Piper said. "It's just hard not to worry."

"Trust me, Piper. There's nothing to worry about this afternoon. Right, Leo?" Phoebe looked at the Whitelighter for confirmation.

"Everything should be fine." Leo leaned over to kiss Piper on the cheek but avoided looking her in the eye. "I'll be back soon."

Piper eyed Leo's dirty shirt. "Aren't you going to—"

Leo dissolved in into a glowing swirl of blue light.

"—change?" Piper frowned at Phoebe. "That was kind of strange, wasn't it?"

Phoebe shrugged. "What difference does it make if he's grungy and sweaty? Nobody will see him except Paige."

"You didn't think he was acting a little evasive?" Piper asked. "Like he was hiding something?"

"Now that you mention it . . ." Phoebe cupped her chin, her eyes narrowing in thought. "But what would Leo be hiding?"

Whatever it is, it can't be good, Piper thought, lapsing into distraught silence. She wasn't sure what was more upsetting: the impending Darklighter threat or Leo keeping secrets.

Chapter
4

Leo materialized in the drawing room on the first floor of the three-story mansion. The Bay Haven formal room was empty, as Paige had thought it would be. Since she had only seen part of the lower level, Leo would have to learn his way around.

Just under an hour had passed since Paige had left the home. Leo headed for the kitchen in the back of the house just in case Todd was still eating the late lunch Ray had promised. The boy was not in sight, but a large man in a stained, white chef's coat and another man in coveralls were seated at a corner table drinking coffee.

"When *will* you have time to check the exhaust fan, Herman?" the chef asked.

"Right now if it's broken, Chuck." Herman blew on a cup of coffee to cool it and took a tentative sip. "But if it's working and just making a funny noise, it can wait. Ray wants the whole back meadow mowed by tomorrow afternoon."

Chuck sighed. "It'll wait, then."

"Thought so." The maintenance man smiled.

"You probably shouldn't put off looking at Sonny's air conditioner, though," Chuck continued. "He said it's blowing hot air and clanking."

"Why is that a problem?" Herman's bland expression soured. "That little jerk is nothing but a scrawny windbag himself."

Chuck shrugged. "Maybe, but his students pass the state achievement tests. Given what he's got to work with here—"

"Do I look like I care?" Herman asked sarcastically.

When the chef stood up, Leo turned toward a set of narrow, enclosed back stairs. He paused to scan a floor plan tacked to a bulletin board with work and activity schedules, notes, and community fliers.

Classrooms, a teacher's lounge, a science lab, and Ray's suite were located in the central area and west wing on the second floor. With the exception of the gardener's quarters over the garage, the rest of the staff was housed in the second-floor east wing. The boys' rooms and TV recreation lounge were on the smaller third floor. The remaining area under the third-floor eaves was used for storage.

Leo emerged on the second-floor landing as a man in shirtsleeves and a tie scurried by. Slim with thick glasses and thinning hair, the man clutched a stack of books under one arm. He mopped sweat off the back of his neck with a handkerchief. Muttering under his breath as though he was trying to commit something to memory, he entered a small office and slammed the door closed.

The teacher, Sonny Hendricks, Leo thought, reading the sign on the office door. In addition to Ray Marino, the teacher, cook, and maintenance man, Bay Haven employed a part-time physical education trainer who also tutored several subjects. Leslie Cray, the visiting nurse and psychologist, was the only female member of the staff. The tutor and nurse did not live at the home.

With the exception of the teacher, the floor was deserted. As Leo moved toward a wide, enclosed staircase leading upward, a commotion erupted on the third floor above. He orbed up.

A furious boy stood by a pile of towels and toiletries he had dropped on the hall floor. A man of average height and weight faced him with unruffled calm.

Ray Marino and Todd Corman, I presume, Leo thought.

"Only a dork would follow all these stupid rules," the boy snarled.

"Do we have a problem, Todd?" Ray asked with chilling calm.

In response, Todd picked up a boxed tube of toothpaste and hurled it down the corridor. It hit a door and fell on the floor beside a wrapped bar of soap.

Leo wasn't the only witness to the showdown between the new boy and the administrator. Three pairs of curious eyes watched from behind three doors cracked just enough to give them a good view of the hall.

The importance of Todd's challenge did not escape Ray Marino, Leo realized. In order to maintain strict discipline, the boy's insolence had to be negated immediately, while Ray had everyone's attention.

Todd folded his arms and jutted out his chin. "I don't have a problem."

"You do now." Ray moved with incredible speed and agility. Before Todd knew what had happened, the administrator had grabbed his arm and hustled him into a vacant room.

Although dismayed by Ray's rough treatment of the boy, Leo decided to reserve judgment. He orbed through the wall, wary and watchful.

Measuring twelve by twelve, the room was furnished with a twin bed, nightstand, four-drawer dresser, desk, and two lamps. The accommodations were luxurious compared to Paige's description of the wards at County Juvenile. Todd didn't recognize his good fortune or didn't care.

"I'm not going to follow your stupid rules," Todd stated evenly, "so you might as well just send me to that government place now."

Interesting, Leo thought, impressed in spite of the boy's defiant lack of respect. Todd had taken the threat of being sent to County Juvenile out of play before the game had barely gotten started.

Two of the other boys ran into a third boy's room directly across the hall. They watched with intense interest as the power struggle between Ray and Todd escalated.

"Sorry, Todd," Ray countered, his tone and demeanor unshaken, "but you're not getting out of here that easily."

Leo raised an eyebrow, equally impressed with the administrator's ability to neutralize Todd's offense.

With a shriek of rage, Todd ripped the bedding off the bunk and stomped on the patchwork quilt. When Ray remained unmoved by the tantrum, the boy stopped and glowered with his fists clutched at his sides.

"You will not eat again until that bed is properly made up," Ray said.

Todd matched Ray's calm with a depth of intensity Leo found disarming. "You can keep me here, but you can't *make* me do anything."

"Maybe not," Ray said with a glance at the three boys standing in the doorway across the hall. "But they can."

"No way," Todd said acidly.

"Bad behavior by one means punishment for all at Bay Haven," Ray explained. "Would you tolerate losing TV and other privileges because one of *them* wouldn't behave or couldn't keep his mouth shut?"

"I wouldn't care one way or the other," Todd retorted. He ignored the other boys, relegating them to non-entities in his world.

Concerned, but fascinated by the verbal duel, Leo was caught off guard when Ray's foot whipped out and kicked the door closed.

Todd didn't flinch. "You don't scare me."

Bravado, Leo wondered, *or is this kid so lost he really doesn't care what happens to him?*

"If I was trying to frighten you, you'd be scared witless right now." Ray's manner implied that he had no compunction about doing whatever was necessary to bend the boy to his will. However, he opted for reason rather than force. "If you're as smart as I think you are, you'll keep that in mind."

Todd's jaw flexed, but he kept quiet.

"I won't insult your intelligence with a lecture about how you'll get farther in life if you give in and learn to cooperate," Ray continued. "That line is for losers."

Leo frowned when he saw the first glimmer of curiosity in Todd's eyes. The boy's interest in the gist of Ray's words was alarming, but there was nothing he could do except listen and report back to Paige.

"But here's something to think about while you're deciding when to make your bed." Ray

stepped toward the door. "The secret to controlling any situation is manipulation of everyone
involved, but successful manipulation of others
begins with self-control."

Todd didn't say anything or move when Ray
left the room. He stared at the closed door.

The anger smoldering in the boy's hardened
gaze gave Leo pause. The hatred Todd had nur-
tured to protect himself from hurt would eventually consume him, unless someone broke
through his defenses and restored his trust.

As Leo orbed home, he sensed that time was
working against Todd Corman.

"I know thirteen years is a long time," Paige told
her contact with the department of motor vehi-
cles, "but we've got to find this guy. He may not
even know he has a son."

After Paige hung up, she made a notation in
Todd's file. The clerk's initial search for Brian
Jamieson had turned up over a hundred leads
throughout the state. She suspected that a shortage of time, funds, and personnel had prevented
county social services from investigating them in
the past. She was busy, too, but she'd find the
time and hopefully she'd find Todd's father. He
was the best solution to Todd's problems.

Unless the guy turns out to be a total jerk, Paige
thought. She wondered if Todd knew more
about the man than he was saying. Every little
bit of information was a clue that might narrow

the search parameters and increase her chances of success.

Paige crossed her fingers when the phone rang, hoping the clerk was ready to fax over a list of B. Jamieson addresses. She tensed when she heard Phoebe on the other end of the line.

"Can you break away to orb home for a few minutes?" Phoebe asked. "Leo just got back from Bay Haven."

"On my way." Paige left her computer on and the Corman file open. If anyone came looking for her, they would assume she'd be right back from a bathroom break. She *was* going to the rest room—to conceal a quick trip home before she returned to her desk.

A tingling vibration coursed through Paige as her body became a photon stream. The particles that were uniquely Paige merged with and folded the ether, a process that transcended the physical world and transported her instantly across space. She coalesced in the center of the attic.

"What took you so long?" Piper teased. She smiled as she looked up from *The Book of Shadows*.

Phoebe sat on the rocker with a memo pad and pen. She sighed wistfully. "There are times I wish I could do that."

"It comes in handy," Paige said. Her ability to orb from one location to another had made her hectic double life much easier to manage. "Right, Leo?"

Leo was staring out the window, deep in thought. He looked back with a puzzled expression. "Hmm?"

"Never mind. Not important," Paige said. "What's going on with Todd?"

Leo hesitated, as though he didn't know how to break bad news.

Paige inhaled anxiously. "Did something happen to him?"

"No, not yet, but . . ." Leo sighed. "I've got to tell you, Paige. I've never encountered a kid who's as devoid of feeling as Todd. It's like he's—"

"Empty?" Paige understood Leo's loss for words. She had felt it too, when she had tried to find a hint of warmth in Todd's dark eyes. "And hopeless?"

"With no regret," Leo added.

"Todd can't be a hopeless case." Piper absently flipped through the pages of *The Book Of Shadows*. "There'd be no point in trying to help him."

"Agreed," Leo said, "but if Todd doesn't start caring about something—besides making everyone around him miserable—soon, he'll forfeit his humanity."

Phoebe leaned forward, resting her elbows on her knees. "The Powers That Be put us in contact with Todd, so there must be something about him that's worth saving."

Paige desperately wanted to believe that.

Todd had been on a one-way journey of self-destruction since his mom had died. He needed saving from himself, and maybe from an unknown Darklighter, too.

"What are you looking for, Piper?" Paige nodded at the book.

"For a reference to specific Darklighters, but there aren't any." Piper scowled. "Which is really annoying . . . and puzzling."

"Yeah," Phoebe agreed. "We know from past experience that individual Darklighters can have their own agendas."

"Beyond killing Whitelighters?" Paige asked.

"Leo vanquished one Darklighter who tried to drive Maggie Murphy to suicide so she wouldn't become a Whitelighter," Piper said.

"And don't forget Alec." Phoebe rocked, agitated. "When Leo tried to protect Daisy from his romantic advances, Alec almost killed him."

"Killing Whitelighters is always the ultimate goal for a Darklighter, whether now or in the future," Leo explained. He held Paige's worried gaze as he perched on a stack of boxes. "By seducing Daisy, Alec hoped to create another evil generation."

"Is there a Darklighter shortage?" Paige hoped her sarcasm hid the deep-seated revulsion and fear she felt.

"Unfortunately there are plenty of rotten people in the world," Leo said. "Darklighters fill their ranks from the bad just as Whitelighters are recruited from the good."

"But there's no such thing as enough evil for evil, Paige." Phoebe's voice hardened with an iron resolve. "The powers of darkness won't be satisfied until good is eradicated."

"But that's not going to happen on our watch." Piper closed the book and glanced at Phoebe. "How are you doing with that Power of Three spell?"

"What spell?" Paige had to get back to the clinic, but it would be easier to concentrate on work knowing that Piper and Phoebe were on top of the Darklighter problem.

Phoebe held up the memo pad. "Since we haven't identified the specific Darklighter, it's a generic spell to vanquish all Darklighters."

As Paige began to orb out, she heard Phoebe add, "I hope."

Chapter
5

"Good morning!" Paige bounced into the kitchen and headed directly for the coffeepot on the counter.

"Leo survived the night, so, yes—it is." Piper wiped a dribble of cereal milk off her chin with a napkin. "A good morning, I mean."

"I've got coffee and doughnuts." Leo held up a half-eaten glazed pastry. "I'm happy."

"Me too, but it doesn't have a darned thing to do with doughnuts." Cole draped his arm over Phoebe's shoulders and grinned.

Phoebe didn't seem to notice. She sipped coffee and scowled at her note pad. Judging from the scratched out lines, she hadn't made much progress with the Power of Three spell.

"What's on everyone's agenda today?" Paige asked, hoping to ease into the topic of Phoebe's vision and Todd.

They had all been on edge waiting for the hour of twilight to pass yesterday. The sun had set and darkness had descended with no word from Ray about Todd and no sign of the mysterious Darklighter. Now they had several hours of daylight to figure out what was going on and how to protect themselves before the sun went down again. *Protect Leo,* Paige corrected herself.

"Library." Cole emptied his coffee cup and stood up.

"Spell." Phoebe tilted her head back for a kiss and turned back to her notes as Cole dashed out the door.

"Garden." Piper hooked her thumbs in the bib straps of her short, denim coveralls. "I've got to finish digging up the lawn and prepping the dirt with stuff to make things grow."

"Todd," Leo said. "Someone has to keep an eye on him."

"And my first official follow-up visit isn't scheduled until tomorrow," Paige said, musing aloud. "I have to admit I'm worried about him. Since the Darklighter vision came from Todd, he must be our innocent."

Nobody argued with that hypothesis. Whoever was in charge of destined meetings made certain that the Charmed Ones connected with those who needed their help.

"Fortunately I can maintain surveillance without being seen." Leo avoided Piper's gaze.

Piper exhaled loudly. "So you'll be prowling

about Bay Haven disguised as the invisible man the next few days."

"Don't worry." Leo kissed Piper's cheek. "No one will know I'm there."

"Who's worried?" Piper playfully pushed him away. "I'm going to the garden store tomorrow to buy tomato and pepper plants. Since you'll be busy lurking, I'll have to put them in the ground myself."

"You're going to *buy* plants?" Phoebe looked up from the pad and blinked. "Why not use seeds?"

"Radishes, carrots, and magical herbs I can wait for." An impish smile played across Piper's face. "I want tomatoes as soon as possible."

"Instant gratification." Paige gave Piper a thumbs-up. "Works for me."

Leo eased back, a look of honest surprise on his face. "You're really not worried?"

Piper rolled her eyes. "I'm worried sick, but what does that have to do with anything?"

"Just asking." Leo held up his hands in surrender.

"At least we know that the Darklighter shows up under specific conditions," Paige said. "There's only a risk just before and after sundown."

"When there's a fog," Piper added.

"Staying out of harm's way might not be quite that simple. We have to go wherever and do whatever's necessary to protect an innocent."

Leaning back, Phoebe glanced at each one in turn. "Even in a twilight fog."

"Actually"—Leo self-consciously cleared his throat—"the fog may not be a reference to the weather. It could be symbolic."

"Since when are my visions studies in symbolism?" Phoebe asked, aghast.

"Is her precognitive power expanding?" Paige rose and poured herself another cup of coffee.

"No," Leo admitted. "This is just the first time fog has been a factor."

Paige saw Phoebe stiffen. Her sister's stunned reaction to Leo's unexpected bombshell wasn't hard to understand. They all depended on Leo's magical expertise and knowledge regarding their powers. Although he wouldn't do anything to compromise their mission or safety, hiding a symbolic aspect of Phoebe's visions was an irritating slight.

"We've always taken the events depicted in my visions literally." Phoebe paused to tone down the caustic edge in her voice. "Now you're saying that what I see doesn't always mean what I think it means?"

"No, that's not what I'm saying." Leo rose and paced as he tried to explain. "Most of the time the fog in your visions is exactly that—a fog or a mist. Water globules suspended in the air and nothing more."

"And the rest of the time?" Phoebe folded her

arms, a defensive gesture that betrayed the hurt she felt.

Paige shifted her gaze between Leo and Phoebe.

Piper stared at her clasped hands, obviously discomforted by Leo's disclosure.

Leo shoved his hands in his pockets. "On rare occasions—"

"How rare?" Paige interrupted.

"Extremely rare," Leo replied patiently. "On extremely rare occasions, the fog represents the mist-and-stone effect."

"Which is?" Phoebe prodded Leo to elaborate when he hesitated.

"An indicator that events in the vision are in flux and subject to change," Leo said.

"What's new about that?" Piper looked up, confused. "We've changed the outcome of a lot of events Phoebe saw in her visions."

"The mist-and-stone effect is different." Leo sat down and paused again, searching for the right words. He settled on a textbook explanation delivered in lecture mode. "The amount of mist or fog in a progression of multiple visions dissipates in direct proportion to the point at which the depicted events become immutable— or set in stone."

Phoebe noticed that Paige and Piper were staring at Leo with the same blank look she had on her face.

"Care to translate that?" Paige fortified herself with a long swallow coffee.

"Okay." Leo rubbed the back of his neck, sighed, and attempted to simplify. "If Phoebe's Darklighter vision is an example of the mist-and-stone effect, she'll have more visions depicting the same event, perhaps with changes. With each successive vision, there will be less fog because the event is becoming more cemented."

Paige squinted at Phoebe. "Are you getting this?"

"I think so." Phoebe reiterated to make sure. "In mist-and-stone visions, the amount of fog is a measure of whether and how much things can be changed."

Leo clapped his hands together. "That's about it."

Paige nodded absently for a moment. "But Phoebe hasn't had another Darklighter vision."

"Not yet, anyway," Phoebe said.

"So the fog could just be fog, right?" Piper asked.

Leo shrugged. "Until Phoebe has a second vision or the first one comes to pass, there's no way to tell."

Paige tried to assuage the apprehension evident on Piper's face. "The main thing is that we know what's coming so we have time to plan for the attack."

"That's a plus, I guess." Piper nodded then

abruptly turned on Leo. "Why are you explaining this now instead of hours ago?"

"For one thing," Leo said, "the elders didn't want Phoebe second guessing her visions when the power was new."

I can't fault the logic behind that judgment, Paige thought. Incorporating a new parameter should be easier now that the visions had become second nature to Phoebe.

Piper's brow knit in agitation. "I mean *before* you orbed off to Bay Haven to check on Todd."

"Because knowing a few hours ago wouldn't have changed my actions, but you would have worried," Leo explained bluntly.

"I don't need to be protected from unpleasant facts, Leo." Piper fumed. "I may fuss about living with the constant threat of our mutual annihilation, but I'm not fragile."

"I know." Leo gently brushed a strand of Piper's hair behind her ear. "But you were having such a good time working on the garden I didn't want to spoil it."

After a moment Piper's scowl softened. "Okay. You're off the hook this time."

"Not quite," Paige said. "There's still that little problem of the Darklighter waiting in the wings."

"A problem that's subject to the fog factor," Piper said.

"A problem we're a long way from solving." Phoebe shook her head and sighed, obviously dismayed. "The accuracy of my visions is unreliable because of the mist-and-stone effect, and I can't get passed word one in the Power of Three spell. A generic Darklighter incantation just isn't going to have the potency of a spell written to spec."

"I'm sure you'll get inspired soon," Paige said. She didn't add that for Leo, a missed deadline was death.

Todd was the last one into the kitchen. He and the other three boys at Bay Haven had just finished seven long hours of class with the resident teacher, Mr. Hendricks. Except for two brief breaks, they had spent the whole day prepping for a state academic evaluation test the next day.

Five years of being shunted from one foster home to another had taught Todd to keep a low profile and his mouth shut until he had a handle on the new people in his life. Although he had only been at the home for one day, it was very obvious that Ray ruled and nobody argued with him, not even the teacher, the maintenance man, or the cook. Aside from the brief exchange the night before, Todd hadn't been around Ray long enough to know how to keep the man off his case. Unlike his many sets of foster parents, it was obvious that Ray didn't care if the kids liked him or not, which gave the administrator the advantage.

Todd hadn't pegged the other kids' strengths and weaknesses yet either.

The two older boys, Ian Gregory and Tyrell Weans, had raced to the rest room on the first break, where they had stayed until Mr. Hendricks called them back to their seats. Hank Marcos had tried to be friendly, but when Todd made it clear he wouldn't answer questions or talk about himself, the younger boy had given up.

During the second break, Ian had made a point of telling him how lucky he was to be at Bay Haven. Ian knew kids who had done time at County Juvenile Detention Center. If their stories of harsh conditions were true, Bay Haven was fun compared to the government kid prison, even though Ray enforced strict discipline. The head man at Bay Haven had dozens of terrible ways to make kids pay for disobeying the rules, but it sounded as though nothing he did would be as bad as going to County.

Frowning as he considered all this, Todd slipped into a chair at the large kitchen table. Hank, Ian, and Tyrell were already seated, waiting for Ray.

"What's your problem, Todd?" Tyrell kicked him under the table. "You don't talk much."

"He's probably starved like the rest of us," Ian said. "We haven't had anything to eat since breakfast, remember?"

Todd grabbed the front of Tyrell's shirt from across the table. His trust in people had been shattered, and he wasn't in the mood to give anyone a break, especially a loudmouth twerp. "Don't *ever* kick me again."

"Or what?" Tyrell jutted his chin.

"Yeah, or what?" Ian's words sounded tough, but he sat in the corner beyond Todd's reach.

Ignoring Ian, Todd glowered at Tyrell. He was certain the bigger boy's in-your-face attitude was a bluff. He only backed off because he saw the cook watching him. "You don't want to find out."

Hank leaned toward Tyrell. "Because anyone who picks on Todd has to deal with *both* of us."

Todd rolled his eyes. "I can fight my own battles, Hank."

"So?" Stung, the small boy slumped back.

Before Todd could speak again, Ray entered. He let the door slam behind him, and his hard gaze flicked from one anxious face to another as he strode across the kitchen.

An almost tangible tension gripped everyone at the table when Ray took a plate from Chuck's hand on his way by. He walked over and set it down in the center of the table. The plate held a club sandwich made of turkey, cheese, lettuce, and tomato. It had been cut into four pieces, which were held together with toothpicks.

"That's lunch and dinner, boys," Ray said. "How you decide to divide it is up to you."

"That's it?" Ian was appalled. "For *all* of us until tomorrow?"

"That's it," Ray said.

The other three boys exchanged glances.

Todd kept his eye on Ray. He suspected that the man never did anything for no reason. There was a point to the exercise.

He wants to see what we'll do, Todd thought. He quickly decided that Ray's first preference was a free-for-all brawl for the prize.

"No rules at all?" Todd asked.

Everyone else shifted uncertainly, not quite sure what Ray wanted, waiting for the next cue.

"Just one. No one tries to grab the sandwich for sixty seconds." Ray turned his wrist, looked at his watch, and held up his other hand. "Starting now."

"There's only one to win this," Todd said to the other boys. "We decide to share it equally."

"Don't think so," Tyrell said. "If that's all we get between now and tomorrow morning, I want it all."

Ian's eyes flashed. "If you want all or nothing, Tyrell, you'll get nothing."

"Are you with me?" Todd glanced at Hank.

"Thirty seconds," Ray said.

When Hank nodded, Todd turned to Ian. "How about you? Part of a sandwich is better than no sandwich, isn't it?"

Ian glanced at Tyrell. Ian was taller with more bulk. He obviously thought he could take the wiry thirteen-year-old Tyrell, but not Todd and Hank, too.

"I'm in," Ian said with a curt nod.

"Bad move." Tyrell stiffened.

"Three, two, one!" Ray lowered his arm.

Ian and Hank sat on either side of Tyrell. As the greedy loner lunged for the sandwich, they each grabbed one of his arms. Todd scooped up the plate and jumped to his feet.

When Tyrell pulled free and swung, Ian ducked. Tyrell's fist slammed into the edge of the table and he doubled over in pain. Hank scrambled away from the table and ran to Todd.

"Get out of here, Tyrell," Todd ordered. "You lose."

"Make me!" Tyrell took another swing at Ian, but the hefty boy moved out of range.

"Out, Tyrell!" Ray thumbed toward the door.

As Tyrell ran from the room, Todd set the plate back on the table. Following his lead, Hank and Ian sat down. Todd handed them each a quarter of the sandwich, and pulled the plate with the remaining half closer.

"What's this?" Ian's unhappy gaze flicked from the triangle of bread and meat to the plate in front of Todd. "How come you get half, Todd?"

"Because I'm the brains of this team," Todd said, aware that Ray was still watching. With the man's respect for power in mind, he met Ian's challenge head on. "You got a problem with that, Ian?"

"Yeah, it's not fair!" Ian huffed.

Todd snatched the quarter sandwich from the

surprised boy's hand and handed it to Hank. "That's what I think about fair, Ian."

"Huh? But I—" Ian's mouth fell open, but when Ray made no move to back him up, he kicked the table leg and stormed out of the kitchen.

"Thanks, Todd!" Hank grinned.

"You earned it," Todd said gruffly. Ray was still watching, and he didn't want the administrator to know he was returning Hank's honest efforts to be a friend with a degree of protection. "Loyalty counts."

Todd started eating without giving Ray another glance, determined not to let what the other kids or the administrator thought of him matter. *Not caring is why Ray has the upper hand*, he realized. That combined with Ray's advice about manipulation and control the night before had made one thing crystal clear.

Indifference *was* power.

Ray Marino entered the library office, locked the door, and paused by the surveillance monitors to check on the boys.

Todd Corman was still in the kitchen with Hank. It had taken a couple hours the night before, but the boy had finally caved and made the bed. After twenty years in juvenile rehabilitation, Ray knew that the boy had not surrendered. He made the best of a bad situation until he could rebel with a chance of winning. It was not the first time Ray had been locked in a contest of wills with a stubborn adolescent. Unfortunately for Todd, he never lost.

Ian Gregory and Tyrell Weans were parked in front of the upstairs TV, sulking. At fourteen, Ian didn't really care for cartoons, but watching them was better than running laps or chores. Tyrell, thirteen and borderline hyperactive with a creative mind, expressed his volatile emotions by drawing his own cartoons.

Eleven-year-old Hank was a master of manipulation with an uncanny ability to game other people. Although Todd had used the younger boy as a weapon against the other two, Hank had chosen the winning team.

Ray sank into his desk chair and glanced at the phone. His prospects had been bleak prior to being offered the administrative job at Bay Haven, and he had accepted in spite of being seriously disillusioned about his career. The ideals that had led him into social work had become irrevocably tarnished. Two decades of dealing with kids who never had the good sense, brains, or ambition to use the second chance he tried to give them was difficult to reconcile.

His success rate had changed for the better since he had taken over at Bay Haven, which was appreciated by the home's wealthy patrons and board. Still, that wasn't enough to make up for too many thankless years and missed opportunities to pursue a more lucrative career. He knew he should feel remorse for taking his frustrations and failures out on the boys in his charge, but he didn't.

Anxious to report on the new kid, Ray picked up the phone and dialed. He did not mince words as he recounted Todd's history and problems.

"Very angry and intense, won't give an inch unless there's some benefit for him." Ray flipped through the file as he delivered the brief. "Todd doesn't seem to care about anything except beating the system and defying authority."

"And your preliminary evaluation is?"

"I haven't known the boy long enough to say with absolute certainty," Ray said. "I think he has potential, if we isolate him from any adverse influences."

"Someone on your staff?"

"His social worker," Ray countered. "Paige means well, but Todd rejected her friendly overtures, and she's more persistent than most."

Ray had nothing against Paige, but meddling was a professional trait. He could almost guarantee that she would make his work with Todd more difficult if not impossible.

"We can have Paige taken off the case," Ray offered. "Her boss at South Bay won't ignore the wishes of Bay Haven's major contributors."

"I'll handle it."

Ray started to agree, but the phone went dead in his hand.

Chapter 6

"Good luck, Paige." Lila clutched a stack of papers to her chest as she left the copy room. She looked disgusted.

"Is something wrong with the machine?" Paige paused in the doorway.

"Chronic paper jams." Lila sighed. "Mr. Cowan called someone to fix it, but the repair guy can't come until tomorrow."

"It's not working at all?" Paige needed copies of several forms and files now. She was already running late and would have to mail them at the post office on her way home.

"It works if you've got the patience of a saint," Lila said with an impish smile. "Rather than try three times to succeed once, I'll wait."

"I have no choice but to deal." Grinning, Paige entered the small room and kicked the door closed. She dropped her files on a table, lifted the copier lid, and placed a page on the glass plate, print side down.

"Okay, let's check this out," Paige muttered as she removed the metal casing on the side. She checked the settings and pressed the print button. Several sheets of paper were pulled into the mechanism, jamming it.

As Paige pulled the paper free, she felt a chill, as though someone was breathing down her neck.

Except no one else was in the room.

Maybe Piper's no-demon-attack jitters are contagious, Paige thought, turning her attention back to the machine. Since it just needed an adjustment, she decided to use a quickie repair incantation. She cast a glance toward the office cubicles to make sure the coast was clear. No one was in sight, but the sense that someone was watching persisted.

Is guilt playing on my nerves? Paige wondered. She had no idea what Leo's bosses looked like, but an image of bearded, glowing old guys peering down in disapproval flashed into her mind. However, since everyone in the office used the copy machine to help people, she didn't think using a magical fix-it solution qualified as personal gain.

Only one way to find out, Paige thought. She composed a short spell, crossed her fingers, and exhaled as she began to recite.

"Tweak the gizmos, gears, and plates so this

machine will duplicate." Paige tensed when a metallic noise emanated from the inside of the machine. She jumped when her files slid off the table.

On guard, Paige scanned the interior of the room. The Darklighter information she had picked up from *The Book Of Shadows* and her sisters suddenly filled her mind. The Whitelighter killers had multiple powers, including the ability to telekinetically move objects, mimic voices, and lurk in an invisible mode.

Paige maintained a level of high alert for several minutes, until Scott stuck his head in the door.

"Are you going to be done soon, Paige?" Scott asked.

"Five minutes." Paige pressed the print button again. When the machine made a perfect copy without jamming, her relief was tainted with anxiety.

Had something been stalking her in the copy room, or was the constant threat of supernatural unknowns making her paranoid?

"Where's Leo?" Phoebe asked Piper as she wandered across the yard. She had drawn a blank on the Darklighter vanquishing spell and hoped some fresh air would clear her head.

"Dumping the dead grass at the county compost site." Piper wiped the sweat off her forehead with the back of her gloved hand.

With her dirt-smudged cheeks and grass-stained knees, Piper looked like she had spent most of the day plowing the backyard with a shovel. She had worn holes in the fingertips of the cloth gloves.

At least she's keeping busy and not freezing or blowing up every little thing that moves, Phoebe thought.

"I suppose being turned into dirt is a fitting end for a lawn." Phoebe looked at the rectangular patch of dirt, trying to envision the garden Piper hoped to grow.

"Then he's going to pop over to Bay Haven again to see how things are going with Todd." Piper continued breaking up dirt clumps with a small three-pronged garden tool.

"I take it he hasn't noticed anything strange." Phoebe squatted to pull a missed tuft of grass out of the dirt.

"Not a thing." Piper sat back on her heels. "The boys were in class all day."

Phoebe shifted uncomfortably. She had no control over her visions, but she still felt responsible for the uncertainty created by the mist-and-stone effect. *Which may or may not apply*, she thought ruefully.

The Power of Three spell had been a lot harder to write than she had anticipated. Worrying about the Whitelighter and not knowing if her visions were accurate had completely disrupted her creative flow.

"Maybe Paige should take the sundown surveillance shift," Phoebe suggested. Leo had mapped out the three floors of the mansion on his various trips, which had reduced the possibility that Paige would orb into occupied space.

"Since Paige is half Whitelighter, Leo wants to minimize her exposure to the danger," Piper explained with a shrug of surrender.

Protecting us is *his job*, Phoebe thought, sighing. Still, assuming the twilight aspect of her vision was correct, she hoped both her Whitelighter relatives got home before the sun went down.

Paige glanced at the dashboard clock as she turned into the mini-mart gas station a few blocks from the post office. It was after six. In addition to dropping off her mail, she had stayed late at work in order to get the rest of her father-finding resources into motion. Everything she could do for Todd had been done. Now she could only wait for results and follow through when appropriate.

Paige sighed as she pulled up to the forward pump. Her innate ability to read people wasn't as precise as Phoebe's glimpses of the future, but it was almost as accurate, and she agreed with Leo's instincts one hundred percent. Young Todd was rushing blindly down a dead-end street that would ruin the rest of his life.

Unless we can convince him that life doesn't have

to be a total bummer, Paige reminded herself. The hardest part of achieving that would come after the Darklighter danger had been removed. Then Todd would have to face and conquer his inner demons.

Paige palmed her debit card and left her purse in the car when she stepped out. The impersonal aspects of auto-pay bothered her on a social level, but the efficiency of conducting the entire fueling process at the pump appealed on another. Free time was a rare commodity now that she was a witch with responsibilities. Anything that saved steps and minutes was a boon.

After the pump accepted her card, Paige lifted the nozzle to fill up for the drive to Bay Haven the next day.

While she waited for the tank to fill, Paige surveyed the people in and around the station. An older man wearing a baseball cap stood behind the counter inside the store. Two teenage girls were buying bags of chips and canned sodas.

A man in a business suit was filling an expensive sedan on the opposite side of the pump Paige was using. He stared at the ground, his attention on his cell phone conversation.

"I know I promised Billy I'd make the game tonight, Claire, but something came up." The man shook his head in exasperation. "And Rickman is an important client."

A woman slipped out of a small SUV parked in front of the sedan. Through an open rear window, she spoke to two young children strapped into car seats. The little girl hugged a worn teddy bear, her face damp with tears. The boy pouted.

"That's Cassie's bear, Michael," the mother said sternly. "Stop teasing her or no TV when we get home."

The young boy stuck out his tongue when his mom turned her back to insert her credit card.

Paige's pump clicked off at just under twelve dollars. She removed the nozzle and held it while she tightened the tank cap. Then, as she lowered the start lever to replace the nozzle, the metal handle began to heat up in her hand.

The unexplained, intensifying heat prompted an overwhelming feeling of cataclysmic peril. Her response was instant and definitive.

Grabbing the door handle of her VW, Paige orbed herself and the car into the far corner of the parking lot just as the gas pump burst into flames.

In the next fraction of a second, the other people at the station began turning to gawk at the fire. Within the same split second, Paige realized they would all be incinerated when the blazing gas pump exploded. She responded instinctively and without hesitation again.

"Pump!" Paige called, her voice muffled by the roaring flames. She swept her arm toward a house on the other side of the highway. A chain link fence surrounded a large, in-ground swimming pool in the backyard. "Into the pool!"

The gas pump dissipated into a thousand points of sparkling light just as it started to blow apart. The few seconds that passed while the inferno orbed from the station into the water seemed like forever to Paige. Since the explosion was already underway, the pump blew up the instant it materialized in the pool. The blast shot a geyser of steam, flame, and debris into the air.

Everything had happened so fast, Paige's sudden, inexplicable relocation to the far reaches of the lot didn't register with the stunned witnesses. They were all focused on the burning pump that had rocketed into the swimming pool.

"Whoa! What the—" The business man blinked as bits of metal and rubber rained onto the destroyed pool and surrounding area. Then he glanced at his empty hand, which had been holding a nozzle attached to the burning pump a moment before. His narrow escape from a fiery death suddenly dawned on him.

"I'm on my way home, Claire." The man tossed his cell phone into the car, jumped in, and started the engine.

Paige watched with relief as the sedan sped clear of the liquid pooling around the cement island. With the pump gone, gasoline gushed from the underground tank.

The other people in the station were not blind to the lingering danger either.

The young mother was already behind the wheel of her car, slamming the door closed. She jammed the stick shift into first, and the car lurched toward the exit.

As Paige slid into her car and turned the ignition key, she saw the girls and the old man burst through the mini-mart door. They ran for a nearby used car lot.

"Get a move on, ladies!" The old man waved the girls to hurry. "This whole darn station could still blow!"

"Just like in the movies!" The shorter girl was flushed with excitement. She talked as she raced for safety. "No one we know is going to believe this, Mandy."

"Who cares? Just run, Donna!" Mandy urged breathlessly.

The wail of distant sirens drew closer.

Satisfied that everyone was clear, Paige peeled out of the parking lot and raced down the highway past an oncoming police car and two fire trucks. With the city's finest and bravest on the scene, she had no reason to stay and every reason to leave.

Although Darryl Morris, a Halliwell family friend in the Police Department, had become an expert at covering up their connection with crimes involving the supernatural, she didn't want to answer any questions about these pyrotechnics.

I have questions, not answers, Paige thought as she stopped at a traffic light. Her hands were white-knuckled on the steering wheel and her legs shook like jelly.

Did I just survive a freak accident, Paige wondered, *or was I the intended victim?*

The tall, lanky figure dressed in shades of black blended into the evening shadows cast by the mini-mart building. He absently traced the jagged scar that ran from the bridge of his nose across a gaunt, left cheek to just below his left ear lobe. The ancient wound was a constant reminder of the tortures he had once endured, the trials he had survived, and the tests he had passed. The man who had slashed his face with a short sword had died horribly by his hand. He had achieved eternal existence.

After centuries of experience in the mortal and magical realms, he was rarely surprised by anything. When he had gone to South Bay Social Services to learn more about Todd Corman's social worker, he had certainly not expected to learn that Paige Matthews was a witch. The spell she had cast to fix the machine was irrefutable proof that she possessed supernatural power.

That, however, had not prepared him for her ability to orb out of harm's way a moment before the gas pump burst into flames.

Scar was as furious as he was perplexed by the unusual development, but he resisted a second attack. Killing a witch in an "accidental" explosion would have removed her from Todd's life without drawing attention to Bay Haven. Now that she had revealed a power no ordinary witch should possess, information was more important than the woman's immediate demise.

Since Scar's Darklighter senses would have detected a pure Whitelighter in such close proximity, he knew Paige had not died to become one of the guardians of good he was empowered to kill.

Scar inhaled sharply, startled again when Paige hurled the exploding gas pump into a swimming pool with a word and a sweep of her hand. For a moment he was as stricken by the fiery display that spewed water, fire, and shrapnel into the air as the station's mortal customers were.

Only one explanation fit what he had just observed: The woman had surely inherited the power to orb from a Whitelighter and her other abilities from the witch he protected. Born of a forbidden union, Paige was an aberration without precedent in his experience.

Scar's hand flexed on the crossbow he held at his side, but he rejected the instinct to slaughter the Whitelighter abomination. For reasons that were not yet clear, the boy's social worker was a magical entity. *By design or coincidence*, he wondered. Either way, her involvement posed questions he had to answer before he indulged his murderous impulses.

Scar studied the slim, pretty woman, missing no nuance of her behavior. Paige had magically removed the burning gas pump to protect the other people at the station, even though her actions risked exposing her true nature. Only now that everyone was safe did she get into her car to leave.

The welfare of others is, without question, her primary concern, Scar reflected. It was also apparent that since Paige had chosen a low-paying career in social services, making money was secondary to helping people.

Is she destined to achieve full Whitelighter status when she dies? Scar wondered, savoring the possibilities. If that premise proved to be true, he would have the pleasure of killing her—twice.

But not just yet, he decided, recalling something Ray had said earlier. Although no mongrel Whitelighter would be allowed to jeopardize the project, the woman's Whitelighter status and desire to help the boy might be used to his advantage.

Since he knew where to find her, Scar let Paige drive away. Denied the immediate satisfaction of killing her, he settled on another target to satisfy his destructive appetite.

Raising his crossbow, Scar loaded a second arrow and set it ablaze with a flick of his finger. He aimed and fired, his mouth pressing into a grim smile as the burning arrow struck another gas pump. Suddenly engulfed in flames, the pump set off a chain reaction that blasted the remaining pumps, cement islands, connecting roof, and fuel storage tanks.

Scar dissolved into a stream of black ash and shimmered out as the mini-mart became an inferno of black smoke, roaring flames, hot metal, and melted glass.

Phoebe lounged in a living-room chair, dangling her legs over the arm and watching the clock. Cole had called just after six to say he was staying late at the library. She was glad he wanted to make a genuine go of it as a lawyer, but she fretted when he was out late. Her concern insulted his male ego, but since he stubbornly refused to accept that he wasn't indestructible now that he was human, she couldn't help it.

"Why should my whole evening be ruined because he has a macho man complex?" Phoebe mumbled. She marked her place in the paperback Paige had lent her, set the book on the table, and reached for the phone.

"Problem, Phoebe?" Piper sat on the sofa beside Leo, watching the nine o'clock news.

Paige was sprawled on the floor clutching a pillow. She cast a quick glance at Phoebe then turned back to the TV.

"Just the mad ramblings of a worried witch," Phoebe retorted. She started to dial Cole's cell.

"Turn that up!" Paige pointed toward the TV as a report about the mini-mart explosion began.

Phoebe dropped the phone, picked up the remote, and hit the volume control.

They had already heard Paige's version of the gas station story. Since Darryl hadn't called, they were certain the police didn't suspect anything strange about the blast and hadn't connected Paige with the incident. All that remained before they could declare an 'all clear' was to find out what the local reporters knew.

"Miraculously, no one was injured when two explosions ripped through this corner gas station earlier this evening." The reporter on location, an attractive young woman with short, straight hair and a wardrobe as serious as her expression, turned sideways. The camera zoomed in on the smoking ruins.

"'Frisco Inferno.'" Piper read the title of the encapsulation scripted at the bottom of the screen. The short lines of typed plot points below the title changed every few seconds.

"Looks like the whole place was demolished," Leo observed.

Paige frowned. "Did she say 'two explosions'?"

Phoebe turned up the volume another notch. The camera was focused on the reporter again. As she continued her report, the camera panned past her toward the obliterated swimming pool on the other side of the road.

"According to several witnesses, the first blast propelled a gas pump across this four-lane highway and into a backyard swimming pool," the journalist said solemnly. "No one was home at the time, and, although the pool was completely destroyed, the house sustained only minor damage."

"Well, that's a relief." Piper looked at Paige. "They all thought the explosion blew the pump across the street just as you hoped."

And no one was hurt, Phoebe thought. She was relieved that Paige and not Cole had been at the station. Since he was no longer capable of shimmering to avoid danger, he would have been flash-fried into charcoal.

"But I still acted without thinking." Paige sat up, hugging the pillow tighter. "What if someone *had* seen my car vanish and reappear in a burst of light?"

"They probably wouldn't have believed their own eyes," Phoebe assured her. "In moments of crisis, the mind often blocks out the unacceptable."

Phoebe had studied eyewitness testimony in one of her psychology classes. In extremely violent situations, people got their facts wrong more often than not.

"Thank goodness." Paige released her chokehold on the pillow and frowned as she tuned back into the newscast.

" . . . second explosion, which destroyed the remaining pumps and the station building, occurred a few minutes later." The reporter's image filled the screen as she concluded. "Although a gas leak or faulty electrical wiring may be to blame, the authorities do not yet know what caused the pumps to catch fire. Rosalyn Stuart, reporting live from—"

Phoebe turned down the sound. "Does this strike anyone else as odd?"

"That nobody noticed Paige orb?" Piper asked, puzzled.

"The assumption that the explosions were accidental," Phoebe clarified. She wasn't suffering from irrational paranoia. The Charmed Ones rarely encountered hazardous situations that were ordinary accidents. "What if Paige was the target?"

"That crossed my mind," Paige said, "but then, I'm a little spooked about the Darklighter you saw in our future."

"Especially Leo's future." Piper shivered. "That's what I get for complaining about the prolonged absence of demonic mayhem instead of enjoying the respite. A Darklighter with his sights set on my husband."

"A Darklighter is a threat to Paige, too." Phoebe swung her legs around and set her feet on the floor.

"Except why would a Darklighter try to blast Paige into burned cinders instead of using his crossbow?" Leo removed his arm from Piper's shoulder, rested his chin on his folded hands, and narrowed his eyes in thought.

"So we wouldn't know a Darklighter was

responsible?" Phoebe voiced the first thing that entered her mind.

"And not get credit for the kill?" Leo shook his head as he straightened. "Not likely."

"Leo's got that right," Piper said. "Every high-level demon who thought it could take us out has just attacked."

Phoebe scowled, marveling at the pervasive arrogance of their evil adversaries. Some were motivated by glory while others underestimated the Charmed Ones' legendary power, despite the overwhelming evidence of their formidable abilities. *Interesting trivia, but entirely off topic,* she thought.

"So then the blazing gas pump *was* an accident." Phoebe looked to Leo for confirmation.

"We can't be certain, but that seems likely," Leo said. "The second explosion happened *after* Paige left the station. That suggests she was just another innocent bystander."

"Maybe," Piper said, "but considering how quiet things have been on the demon front the past several days, we shouldn't dismiss the possibility of a supernatural enemy."

"Could I make a suggestion?" Phoebe asked, but she didn't wait for an answer. "We can sit here what-iffing all night and still not know anything more than we do right this second."

"True," Paige said, nodding. "It's not like anything we've discussed is going to help me sleep a whole lot easier."

"Me either, but I don't think worry-free Zs was Phoebe's point." Piper pressed closer to Leo.

"The point is this: If one or all of us are on some bad guy's to-kill list," Phoebe went on, "whoever it is will try again. In the meantime, there's not much we can do except stay alert."

"We're not entirely clueless, though." Paige drew up her knees and rocked slightly. "My close encounter with a big bang barbeque might have been an accident, but Leo's future face-off with a Darklighter won't be."

"Well, yeah." Phoebe winced. "There is that."

Being the messenger of imminent disaster was always hard, but it was harder when the news directly endangered someone in the family. *Still, forewarned is forearmed,* Phoebe told herself, *and because of the vision, Leo won't be blindsided.*

"I've handled Darklighters before," Leo said.

"And it's high time I did." Paige suddenly tossed the pillow aside, as though casting off her insecurities.

Phoebe wasn't fooled by her sister's show of courage. Paige was terrified of the dark beings that hunted and executed Whitelighters. Although Phoebe felt certain her sister wouldn't succumb to the fear, prudence demanded that she keep the young witch's dread in mind.

Invisible and silent, Scar watched and listened from a corner of the room. Given the topic of conversation and the information he had acquired, his surveillance of the witches in their home could not have been better timed.

The three women were not just weekend wiccans with a high affinity for the magic arts. They were the Charmed Ones, the most powerful witches of all time.

And they know that a Darklighter haunts their future, Scar thought.

For a brief moment after realizing their identity, Scar had cursed himself for not killing Paige at the gas station. Then, upon further reflection, he knew his instinct to wait had been correct. Dealing with the surviving sisters' vengeance for Paige's death would have created an unnecessary, premature complication.

Now that he knew the Charmed Ones' destiny was entangled with his and the boy's, he could compensate for the witches' interference and powers.

And incorporate the demise of two Whitelighters into my plans, Scar thought as he shimmered out.

Chapter
7

Scar watched from the trees as Ray led four boys onto the field that separated the mansion's manicured lawns from the surrounding forest. His eyesight was not drastically impaired in the dark lit only by a half-moon, but acute night vision was not his most potent resource. Although he had learned much about the Charmed Ones through observation, he could tell more about the young humans by the way they moved, what they said, and how they reacted to the late night hazing.

"Stop here," Ray ordered sharply. There was no trace of sympathy in his tone, no flexibility in his stance.

All four boys halted abruptly, but that was the only similarity in their response.

Earlier, Scar had instructed Ray to awaken the boys, drag them from bed, and march them outside into the dark without a word of explanation. How they perceived and dealt with the unexpected and unpleasant turn of events was the first test of their suitability.

"I'm cold." Ian Gregory, the oldest, wrapped his arms around his chest and hunched over. His protective posture punctuated the distress he felt. "I don't think the County—"

"Shut up," Ray snapped.

Scar was not surprised when Ian clamped his mouth closed and stared at Ray through wide, frightened eyes. Ian's aversion to physical activity was evident in his bulky build and lack of muscle tone. That, however, was not what disqualified him as a candidate for Scar's project. The boy was a whiner who was too quick to back down.

"Wimp." Tyrell Weams punched the redheaded Ian in the stomach, eliciting a yelp of surprise. Laughing, Tyrell mimicked a boxer's footwork and threw another punch.

"Don't!" Ian shielded his face with his hands.

Before Tyrell could press the fight, Ray moved behind him and grabbed his arms.

"Stand still," Ray barked.

"Let me go!" Twisting his thin body, Tyrell struggled to pull free. The tighter Ray held him, the harder he fought.

Scar's upper lip curled back in disgust at Tyrell's lack of thoughtful self-discipline. The teenager had no hope of fighting free of Ray's grip, but he was too driven by blind instinct to consider his options and plan an escape. Tyrell could have won the contest of wills by standing still as the administrator had demanded and making a break for it after Ray let go. That, however, was irrelevant. A boy who had no command of reason was worthless for Scar's purposes.

When Tyrell finally stopped struggling, Ray released his arms and pushed him away.

"Jerk," Ian whispered.

Humiliated, Tyrell pulled back his fist to take it out on Ian. "What did you say?"

"Knock it off, guys," the youngest boy pleaded. An opportunist who switched allegiances without compunction to gain advantage, Hank Marcos had never been on Scar's list of potential candidates.

"Stuff it, Hank," Tyrell snarled.

Hank turned to the fourth boy, who stood slightly apart from the group. "Make them quit it, Todd."

The Darklighter's gaze skimmed past Hank to Todd Corman.

The new boy showed no emotion regarding the late night, cross-country trek or the personality conflicts. Standing tall, his expression neutral, Todd appeared totally detached.

Todd shrugged. "Not my problem, Hank."

"If they fight, Ray will take TV away from *all* of us," Hank hissed.

"Five laps around the field," Ray said, ending the discussion. "All of you, starting now."

"Five!" Ian sagged.

Tyrell's eyes flashed. "Forget it."

"Ten," Ray countered.

"Nice going, Tyrell," Ian grumbled as the two boys started to run.

Scar noted that Todd had already moved out with Hank following on his heels. If Todd cared that the younger boy looked up to him or that Tyrell and Ian's arguments had added laps, he didn't show it. Todd's disdain and self-imposed isolation were only two of several traits that made him a prime candidate for the Darklighter recruitment project.

Just as truly selfless people became Whitelighters after they died, those with hardened hearts and no tolerance for mercy became Darklighters. Scar had reveled in the glory of his violent life as a gladiator and accepted death without fear. His ensuing existence as an underworld agent of hate and destruction was his reward for the pain and misery he had brought to the arena.

As the boys passed Scar's position, Todd put on a burst of speed to widen the distance between himself and the others.

"Wait for me, Todd!" Hank called out breathlessly, but Todd ran without looking back.

They are nothing to him, Scar observed. His dark eyes gleamed with approval for the protégé he would soon enlist. Ray's initial assessment of Todd Corman had been correct. The orphaned boy fit Scar's candidate profile perfectly.

A rare find, Scar thought. Most delinquents and young street criminals did not qualify as future Darklighters. History was rife with the terrible deeds of ruthless tyrants, but few men were so thoroughly evil that every trace of goodness had been purged from their being. Of those few, the insane megalomaniacs were also weeded out. The immense power of the underworld could not be entrusted to erratic personalities.

In the arenas of ancient Rome, Scar had been known as Stratorius the steady one. Born of warrior blood and tempered by a gladiator's unforgiving life, he had become a creature of undiluted evil, fulfilling a destiny for which he had always been predisposed.

The twenty-first century urban environment was a pathetic breeding ground by comparison. Even so, operating on the premise that certain boys could be cultivated into adults that lived to maim and kill, Scar intended to create an army of Darklighters who were unshakably loyal to him.

A faction unlike any the underworld has ever known, Scar vowed as his hand closed into a fist of resolve.

By their very nature, Darklighters were too independent, arrogant, and single-minded in the quest to perpetuate evil and kill Whitelighters to work together effectively. Consequently, there had never been a cohesive, competitive faction of Darklighter power, a niche Scar intended to fill.

Darklighters that had been primed to respect his leadership and trained to kill without remorse from an early age could ultimately eradicate Whitelighters.

Over the millennia, many had plotted to eliminate all Whitelighters. Some had attempted it. None had succeeded.

I will not fail, Scar thought as he watched the boys race by Ray at the end of the darkened field. Defeat was not in his makeup. No man had ever beaten Stratorius, Rome's favorite in the games during the first-century reign of the Augustans. In the end, three male lions had brought him down with fang and claw.

Nineteen hundred years later, Scar could still hear the crowd screaming his name as he walked into the Colosseum for the last time. . . .

"Stratorius! Stratorius!"

Scar strode into the new, massive arena that dominated the landscape of Rome. Dust billowed around his sandaled feet, and the foul stench of old battles assaulted his nose. This time, his final appearance for the glory of Rome and the pleasure of the frenzied crowd, he carried no weapon and wore no armor.

A free man, he had audaciously ignored Caesar's command for mercy and slaughtered the ruler's prized gladiator with a single, defiant stroke of his sword.

As punishment, the undefeated Stratorius had been condemned to die the ignoble death a slave—not by a man's spear or sword, but in the jaws of wild cats.

As Scar walked, the beasts lunged against the chains that tethered them to stone pillars. Starved for three days, the lions bared sharp teeth and roared in anticipation of ripping him apart. He ignored them, remembering the triumphs of his life with a fierce pride that no Caesar could diminish or destroy.

Captured and enslaved at age twelve, his refusal to submit had made him a poor servant. His feisty nature had, however, made him perfect practice fodder for the gladiators in training at his master's compound. He alone was not surprised by the natural abilities that allowed him to elude injury at the hands of older and stronger men. His physical prowess and stubborn defiance had finally won him the status of gladiator.

Scar paused in the center of the Colosseum and surveyed the thousands who had come to witness his death.

"I fought for you!" Turning his back to Caesar, he spoke to the crowd. His voice echoed off stone as he raised a fist to the sky. "I die for *you!*"

The mob rose as a single entity, cheering. "Stratorius! Stratorius!"

He had earned their adoration and praise. Driven by a burning ambition, he had developed superior strength and cunning during two years of intense training. He was seventeen when he fought his first gladiatorial duel.

His opponent had slashed his face.

He had driven a spear though the other man's heart.

He had fought often and well since then, earning his freedom when he had survived five years in the games. After that, knowing nothing but the art of battle in the arena, he had continued to fight as a free man.

Now, as he always did before battle, he touched his disfigured face. Unlike the men who had fallen under his sword, the name Scar did not make the cats tremble in terror. They were animals, concerned only with satisfying a savage hunger.

Scar squared his shoulders and held his head high as the beasts were unleashed. He could not possibly survive the ordeal, but he could thwart Caesar's vengeful desire to humiliate and beat him.

He did not cower, struggle, or strike when the lions attacked. He stood his ground, embracing the beasts and death with the same calm, unwavering sense of inevitability that had ruled his life.

Scar died with his name thundering in his ears.

"Stratorius! Stratorius!"

When he awoke in the nether world of supernatural evil, he accepted his remarkable fate without question. Whole and healed, except for the facial scar that had defined his previous existence, he kept the blemish and his name as a reminder.

Neither life nor death had beaten him. Nothing ever would.

Paige sat in the attic rocker watching Piper flip through *The Book Of Shadows* again. Leo stood behind Piper, massaging her shoulders as he peered over them to study the book.

Too strung out to sleep, Paige, Piper, and Phoebe had returned to the attic after the local newscast ended at ten. Leo had arrived a few minutes later via an orb detour to Bay Haven. His report that Todd and the other boys were asleep in their rooms had put Paige's mind at ease—to a degree.

It was past midnight. They had spent the last two hours going over everything they had discussed before and during the news. As Phoebe had predicted, they didn't know any more now than they had earlier.

"So has the invisible hand written anything since we checked the book the last time?" Phoebe asked, referring to the new pages and passages that Halliwell ghosts added to *The Book Of Shadows*, usually as they were needed. She sat cross-legged on the floor with her memo pad.

"Nope." Piper answered without looking up and continued to turn pages. "How are you doing?"

"Our muse must be on vacation." Phoebe tapped the small pad with a pencil.

"What's wrong?" Leo asked.

"Writer's block, but don't worry. I promise we'll have a Darklighter vanquishing spell when we need it." Phoebe stuck the eraser end of the pencil back in her mouth and resumed her nervous gnawing.

Paige empathized with Phoebe's frustration. Her vision had brought the Darklighter threat to their attention. Being stuck on the Power of Three spell to vanquish the Whitelighter killer probably made her feel as though she was letting them down twice. Phoebe was wrong about that, but like most students of psychology, she was too close to her own head to sort it out.

Paige understood because she felt the same way about Todd. She hadn't created his problems, but once she had been assigned to his case, she felt responsible for everything connected with it. She pulled the business card she had tried to give the boy out of her pocket and rocked forward with a heavy sigh.

"Problem?" Leo shifted his gaze from Phoebe to Paige.

"Just worried about Todd," Paige answered.

"In general or because he's going to see Leo and the Darklighter fight?" Piper closed the book and pulled Leo down into a pile of pillows. She rubbed her lower back. "This part could use some loosening up."

"Back rubs are my specialty." Leo made an exaggerated show of loosening up his fingers.

"Both, I guess," Paige said, steering the conversation back to Todd. In addition to getting an educated opinion about the boy, she hoped that taking Phoebe's mind off the spell for a few minutes would help her get back on track. "But since Darklighters don't target human boys, the in general part is probably more important to him."

"Something specific?" Phoebe dropped the pencil and memo pad in her lap.

"You tell me." Paige held the business card so the others could see the number written on the back. "I tried to give him my phone numbers before I left Bay Haven so he wouldn't feel like I was running out on him."

"Why do you still have the card?" Piper asked.

"Todd wouldn't take it." Sighing, Paige put the card on the table beside the rocker. "I thought he was starting to trust me, but he turned his back, like he wanted to drive me away."

"I don't think that's what he was doing," Phoebe said.

"What then?" Paige cast a hopeful glance at her sister. Although Phoebe's psychology expertise was strictly academic, she had an innate understanding of human nature that transcended clinical experience.

"Considering his pattern of emotional and destructive outbursts," Phoebe began, listing the offenses, "running away, breaking things, causing as much trouble as possible, he could be subconsciously testing everyone *he* cares about."

"Testing for what?" Piper looked skeptical. "The tolerance limit of the average adult?"

Phoebe shook her head. "He may be hoping to find someone who loves him so much that *nothing* he does, no matter how awful, can make them leave."

Paige frowned, wondering if Phoebe could possibly be right. Recalling notations she had read in Todd's file, his behavior during the five years he had been in foster care seemed to fit the theory.

"I think you might be onto something, Phoebe." Paige stood up, pacing as she talked. "From his first foster home on, everything was fine while Todd was settling in and getting to know his new families. Then all of a sudden, he'd turn into a one-kid reign of misery and mayhem."

"Probably after he started to feel comfortable and accepted," Phoebe added.

"But if everything was fine and he wanted

people to care, why would he deliberately try to wreck it?" Leo looked genuinely perplexed.

"Perhaps because he didn't believe it would last and wanted proof he could hold on to. He, uh . . ." Phoebe hesitated, taking a deep breath. "He might even feel that his dead mother abandoned him too."

Piper instantly picked up on the subtle change in Phoebe's demeanor. "Is that how you felt about our mom, Phoebe? Like she deliberately abandoned you?"

"No." Phoebe looked up sharply. "Did you?"

The question surprised Piper, but she responded without pause. "No, she didn't die and leave us on purpose any more than Todd's mother did."

"That's right." Phoebe smiled to dispel any lingering tension. "But Todd was too young to rationally handle the loss."

"You were younger," Piper pressed, as though she needed additional assurance that Phoebe harbored no subconscious animosity toward their mother.

"*Too* young to understand." Phoebe leaned over and squeezed Piper's hand. "I also had family—Grams and sisters who loved me just as much as I love them."

"Todd doesn't have anyone," Paige mused softly.

She had felt completely alone when her adoptive parents had been killed. *And responsible,*

Paige thought, *even though the accident wasn't my fault*. The trauma of Kari Corman's sudden death would have had just as profound an effect on Todd's seven-year-old psyche.

"Any luck trying to locate Todd's father?" Leo asked.

"Not yet." Paige frowned, worried.

"Here's hoping you succeed," Phoebe said. "Todd's father may be the one person in the world that can make a significant difference in his life."

"For better or worse," Paige said. "What if I find Brian Jamieson and he doesn't want to acknowledge his son?"

"That kind of rejection could be bad." Phoebe frowned. "Most people never have to face it, but there's something in everyone's life that can push him over the edge to a point of no return."

Paige nodded, stricken by another possibility. "For Todd, that something might be our mysterious Darklighter."

As Todd started his tenth lap around the field, his legs ached and his lungs labored for air. He stumbled over a rock but caught himself before he fell. He had never been so tired, but nothing would make him quit. He'd crawl through the dirt and weeds on bare hands and knees to finish before he'd give Ray Marino the satisfaction of breaking him.

Todd could see Hank just ahead, a scrawny

silhouette in the dim moonlight dragging his feet in a listless jog. The puny eleven-year-old was two laps behind.

Empowered by determination, Todd summoned another burst of energy and ran ahead of the younger boy. Snubbed when Todd had passed him the first time, Hank didn't bother to speak now.

Good, Todd thought with a glance toward Ian and Tyrell. The older boys were half a lap behind him and fading fast.

"Ian! Tyrell! Move it!" Ray yelled. "Nobody goes inside until everyone finishes."

The two boys sped up for a few seconds but couldn't sustain the increased pace.

Todd wondered if Ray would put the pressure on Hank. After they had started running, the administrator had focused on the two troublemakers and ignored him and the younger boy. If Hank was lucky, Ray had lost track of how many laps he had completed.

The hair on the back of Todd's neck bristled suddenly. He frowned, overwhelmed by the creepy sense that someone was watching from the forest. He shook off the feeling, chiding himself for letting his imagination run wild just because it was dark. The only creatures lurking in the trees were birds, bugs, and small animals.

Ray's the one who really creeps me out, Todd thought. The man's cold calm scared him in a way that none of his angry, screaming foster dads ever had. That was why he had thought about Ray's words after the man left his room yesterday. Nobody messed with someone they feared.

"The secret to controlling any situation is manipulation of everyone involved," Ray had said, "but successful manipulation of others begins with self-control."

Todd suspected that was something Ray told kids to make them behave, but it was still good advice. Ray was tough, but he respected anyone he thought was just as tough.

So I'll just have to be tougher and *smarter*, Todd decided, gritting his teeth against a pain in his side. Challenging Ray's authority like Ian and Tyrell wouldn't keep the administrator off his back, but pretending to cooperate might.

For now, Todd would do whatever Ray asked without question or delay. That wouldn't be much fun for someone who liked to bully kids. Sooner or later, Ray would get bored and start picking on Ian and Tyrell again.

I hope, Todd thought as he slowed down. *Better them than me.* Weary and winded, he stopped, placed his hands on his knees, and bent over to catch his breath.

Ray glared at him. "It took you long enough."

Todd nodded and spoke between gasps. "Next time . . . I'll be . . . better. Promise."

Grunting, Ray snapped his gaze toward Hank. "Two more, boy."

Hank was too scared to argue or answer. He looked at Todd for help.

"Run, walk, or crawl," Ray went on, "you're going to finish, Hank. I don't care if it takes all night. Quitters don't get anywhere in this life."

Todd stared at the younger boy. He was certain that Hank's instant "friendship" was a defensive move against Ian and Tyrell, who picked on him without mercy. However, until siding with Hank became a liability, Todd would play along.

But not where Ray was concerned.

"You heard the man, Hank," Todd said bluntly. *"Walk."*

Hank hesitated, then sighed and trudged away.

From the corner of his eye, Todd caught Ray watching him. He hoped the man didn't think he had gone soft on Hank. If Ray thought he cared about anyone, he could use it as leverage against him.

Not gonna happen, Todd vowed. He had found a stray dog when he was ten, and his foster father at the time had let him keep it. After he had gotten attached to Sparky, the man had used the threat of taking the dog to the pound to control him. Todd had been so afraid for Sparky he had found the dog another loving home himself.

After that, he had sworn not to care about anything ever again. Showing his feelings just gave his enemies more power over him.

"Parade rest while you're waiting, Todd." Ray stood with his feet apart and his hands clasped behind him. "Like this."

Todd obeyed without comment.

"Self-discipline," Ray added before he turned to yell at Ian and Tyrell when they collapsed in breathless heaps.

Todd stared into the woods, tuning out Ray's harsh words and reinforcing his resolve. In a way, it was too bad he hadn't gotten Ray's advice about how to control stuff sooner. He had thrown tantrums, run away, and broken things because he had always been too anxious to let everyone know how he felt.

And that *didn't do me any good,* Todd reflected. Not one adult in the past five years had ever *really* listened. They had just walked away because he was too much trouble.

Todd's only consolation was that he wouldn't always be a kid people could push around and shove aside. One day he'd make them all pay for hurting him, even Paige. For a moment that morning he had thought she was different from the other caseworkers he had known, that she really cared what happened to him.

"Man, was I wrong about that!" Todd huffed under his breath, cursing himself for almost being taken in. Nobody who cared would have left him with someone like Ray.

Does Paige know that Ray makes kids run laps in the middle of the night? Todd wondered. He probably should have kept her business card, especially since she had written her home phone number on the back. *Too late now,* he thought with a sigh.

When Hank finally finished, Ray ordered everyone to head back to the mansion. Todd was so tired, he walked with his gaze on the ground, concentrating on the simple act of putting one foot in front of the other. When Ray led them through a stone archway into a courtyard, he was caught by surprise. They had left the house through a side door off the kitchen.

"What is this place?" Hank asked with a quiver in his voice.

Todd studied the spooky surroundings.

The courtyard had been built into a steep slope a short distance behind the mansion. A large double door made of heavy timbers in the opposite wall suggested that a passageway connected the courtyard with the house at the basement level.

Tangles of dead vines draped twelve-foot high walls made of huge stone blocks. Rivulets of water ran from cracks in the moss-covered stones and pooled on a flat stone floor. A carpet of leaves, wet and dry, cushioned the thud of their shoes on the hard surface. Black and brittle plants adorned raised stone planters, the remains of the once flourishing gardens. A dead tree in the center raised leafless branches to the star-studded sky, as though pleading to be lifted from its grave. Curved stone benches and a headless cement statue of a deer completed the bleak tableau.

"Great spot for a Halloween party," Tyrell quipped.

"Yeah," Ian retorted. "If you're inviting ghouls and ghosts."

"Like I said, great place—" Tyrell stopped talking when Ray opened the double door. The sound of creaking, rusted hinges was amplified by the courtyard acoustics and midnight silence.

Hank gasped and grabbed Todd's arm.

"Don't." With an eye on Ray, Todd shrugged loose of Hank's grip and stepped away.

Ian balked outside the doorway. "I'm not going in there first."

Todd stared into a dark corridor that was lit by a single, unshielded lightbulb. Spiderwebs and cobwebs were strung along the brick ceiling and walls. The sound of water dripping echoed from the dark that obscured whatever lay beyond.

"I'll go." As Todd moved into the tunnel, he thought he saw Ray smile. Whatever questions that raised were forgotten when the acrid odor of damp decay stung his nose. Gagging, he quickened his pace.

Stumbling behind Todd, Ian sank to his hands and knees when they emerged into a musty cellar. "I'm going to be sick!"

"Do it in the sink over there." Todd pointed to

a deep, double laundry tub under a small, dirt-encrusted window in the wall to the right. A large industrial washer and dryer stood next to the tub.

A quick survey of the underground room seemed to prove that his theory about the mansion basement was correct. Pipes and valves ran along the ceiling, and shelves full of jars and miscellaneous junk lined the far wall. Boxes and trunks were stacked in a corner under a set of wooden stairs. The light cast by two bare, dusty bulbs enhanced the gloomy atmosphere.

"The shower is over there." Ray pointed toward a tiled alcove that measured six feet by eight. Four sets of showerheads and water valve knobs were spaced along the left side. "Shower first, then sleep."

Tyrell peered into the alcove. "I don't see any soap." "You don't need soap." Ray stepped into the stall and turned the four water knobs.

Cold water only, Todd noticed.

"Whatever." Tyrell pulled off his T-shirt. "I just want to get back to bed and sleep for a zillion hours."

"Me too." Ian plunged into the tiled stall and shrieked. He quickly jumped out. "That water's freezing!"

"No shower, no sleep," Ray said.

Although Hank hadn't been exposed to the cold water, his teeth chattered. "How long?"

"Three minutes." Ray glanced at Todd after the other three boys were in the shower.

Todd stared back, his eyes narrowed with defiance. Although he had just decided to cooperate, his self-respect suddenly seemed more important than escaping Ray's wrath.

"Men who conquer physical discomfort can't be controlled," Ray said in the same matter-of-fact tone he had used to make his point about manipulation earlier.

Inside the shower, Tyrell swore.

Ian stamped his feet and patted his arms, his verbal shiver sounding like a rumbling motor.

Hank clenched his teeth and squeezed his eyes shut.

Todd suddenly wondered if the night's ordeal was some kind of sadistic test Ray had cooked up to separate the wimps from the tough guys. If so, the others weren't passing with honors, but they were getting through it.

Realizing he had no choice, Todd slipped out of his clothes. He didn't want to deal with Ian and Tyrell dumping on him for being too proud or too chicken to take a cold shower.

Besides, as much as Todd hated to concede anything, Ray was right again. People who couldn't be intimidated couldn't be broken. The icy water could be endured if he just concentrated on something else.

Stepping under the stinging spray, Todd

stood quietly with his arms at his sides, braced to weather the cold. He focused his gaze on a cracked tile and his mind on his misery.

He thought about Paige, the only person he knew who could rescue him from Ray.

Chapter
8

"Hi, Ray. It's Paige Matthews." Paige had arrived at the clinic to find a voice-mail message from Ray canceling her one o'clock visit to Bay Haven that afternoon. "I was surprised to hear from you so early today."

The follow-up was standard procedure whenever a kid was placed in a new environment. Although these visits were occasionally postponed by unforeseen circumstances, she had to see Todd without delay. In addition to the supernatural threat in the boy's future, Phoebe's theory regarding his aloof attitude—that no one cared enough to stick with him no matter what—felt right.

"Sorry my message was so abrupt," Ray said. "It's been a little hectic around here this morning. The department of education sent a rep to conduct academic evaluation tests on all the boys."

"Todd's arrival was well timed, then." Paige took an assertive approach. "I can rearrange my schedule to drop in later this afternoon to see him and consult with you on his test results."

"At the risk of overstepping my bounds, that's probably not a good idea." Ray sighed, as though hesitant to say what was on his mind.

Is he concerned about my ego or is he hiding something? Paige wondered.

"Todd and I have had a couple strained moments," Ray explained, "but he's already gotten over it. He's settled down with remarkable speed considering his background."

Paige nodded, noting that Ray's account reflected what Leo had observed. That didn't relieve her anxieties, though. Todd had a history of trying to get along at first, so his behavior wasn't unusual.

"Any elements that aren't part of the normal Bay Haven routine might interfere with his acceptance of the new circumstances," Ray went on. "Todd's been in foster homes before, not an institution with set rules and regulations."

"Yes, I see your point," Paige lied. "Just keep me posted on his progress."

Paige's stomach twisted into a knot after she hung up. Although the reasoning behind Ray's thinking seemed sound, it didn't quell her uneasiness. On a purely professional level, she couldn't afford to antagonize the administrator of Bay Haven. But she couldn't accept his assessment of Todd without an in-person validation, either.

Paige wasn't comfortable having to investigate behind Ray's back, but he had left her no choice. If she did find anything amiss at Bay Haven, the clinic could officially pursue established procedure to correct it.

Paige called another client to reschedule a morning meeting for that afternoon and made a notation in her appointment book. She did not erase the visit she had penciled in for Todd at Bay Haven.

If anyone wonders, they'll assume I'm on my scheduled follow-up call, Paige thought as she headed for the door, *not orbing into the home to spy.*

Rather than take additional time to drive home, Paige drove to the mall where an unattended car wouldn't attract attention. She parked the VW bug in a remote corner, made sure no one was nearby, and ducked down. Although she didn't have the luxury of remaining invisible like Leo, she had the benefit of Leo's exploration of the Bay Haven mansion the day before. She concentrated on the second floor where the classrooms were located and orbed into a supply room.

Although the chances were slim to none that anyone would be getting supplies at precisely that moment, Paige was on guard as she materialized. In the dim light coming through a high, narrow window, she instantly ascertained that she was alone and took a moment to get her bearings.

Paige hadn't met the resident teacher, Sonny Hendricks, but she knew him by reputation. The meticulous order of the boxes of school supplies and books stacked on wall-to-wall shelves reflected his precise, bookish personality.

Carefully cracking the door, Paige glanced down an empty hallway and paused to listen. Nothing disturbed the morning stillness except the rustling of papers and a muffled cough.Recalling the second floor layout Leo had described, Paige opened the supply room door wider. The door into the room directly across the hall was open, giving her a clear view of the classroom between the door and the far wall.

Todd and two other boys sat at desks, bent over test papers. If the fourth boy was in the room, he was sitting off to the side out of her line of sight.

A scarred man wearing a dark sweater sat behind a large desk in front of the students. Since he did not fit Leo's description of Sonny Hendricks, Paige assumed he was the rep from the department of education Ray had spoken of.

The man looked up from the book he was reading. His gaze lingered on the boys for a moment before it slipped back to the printed page.

Todd straightened and rubbed the back of his

neck, then relaxed and put pencil to paper again.

If the classroom was an accurate indicator, nothing untoward was happening at Bay Haven.

As Paige quietly closed the supply room door, she felt a little foolish for suspecting Ray Marino of ill intent or lying. *But only a little,* she thought. For a Charmed One, concerned folly was infinitely more prudent than operating on false assumptions. Lives were at stake.

With that in mind, Paige decided to explore the mansion. Although Leo's detailed information about the staff's schedules and the floor layout was helpful, it wasn't an adequate substitute for a firsthand recon.

Forty minutes later she had discovered that Ray and the resident teacher were working at computers in their respective offices, the chef was cooking, and the maintenance man was mowing the lawn. Since Todd was safe and nothing seemed amiss, her time would be better spent trying to track down his father. Ducking into the formal front drawing room, Paige left Bay Haven in a stream of light.

"Half an hour." Scar towered over the boys as he strode between desks toward the door. They seemed to sense that he was a person of importance at the home and not a mere teacher. "Don't be late getting back."

Scar paused in the doorway and looked back. Although he had just dismissed the class for a recess, the disgusting little urchins were so intimidated, not one had dared move while he was still in the room. Todd alone had met his gaze. Only for a second, but that was long enough to prove the boy had backbone.

"Believe me," Scar said in a low, ominous voice, "you will regret it."

Todd shifted position to look at him again. His brown eyes gleamed with the calculating fury of a cornered predator waiting for the right moment to strike.

Scar held his stare until the boy looked away. Then the Darklighter turned and swept down the corridor.

Sonny Hendricks, a pathetic excuse for a man, came out of his office with his nose in a book. When the teacher glanced up and saw Scar, he flattened himself against the wall.

Scar snarled as he passed, which sent Sonny scurrying to safety in his office. The door slammed and the deadbolt clicked into place as the Darklighter turned into the stairwell and shimmered out. When he materialized by the desk in the downstairs office, Ray jumped.

"Weren't you expecting me?" Scar's contempt for his human partner hovered under a thin veneer of sarcasm.

"I expected you to use the door like everyone else," Ray said. "What if someone on the staff or one of the kids sees you pop out of thin air?"

Scar scowled. "Do you think I'm that careless?"

"No, of course not." Ray coughed softly, as though realizing it was a major mistake to question Scar's actions.

Not for the first time, Scar wondered if he could have found a less annoying human partner. *Probably not,* he thought.

Once he decided to create a faction of Darklighters, Scar had scoured the mortal world for a source of young candidates. It quickly became apparent that the most accessible prospects were not suitable. The poor, abandoned, and hopeless souls that survived on third-world streets were cunning, but in a feral way that defied corruption. Theft, murder, and betrayal were often essential to their survival, which diminished the potency of the crimes. His Darklighter prospects had to demonstrate an affinity for self-serving cruelty independent of the basic needs.

The boys that ended up in corrective institutions had rejected the benefits of civil society in favor of their aberrant, often malicious behavior. In order to have the access necessary to recruit them, it had been necessary to enlist mortal help. The nature of the job demanded someone who had no scruples and a price.

Bay Haven was ideal because the privately funded home for delinquent boys was not subject to intense government scrutiny. More importantly, however, was that Ray Marino was the administrator. The principles that led the man into juvenile rehabilitation had become irrevocably tarnished. Twenty years of dealing with kids who never had the good sense, brains, or ambition to use the second chance he tried to give them had primed Ray for Scar's purposes. Money had sealed the deal.

"How are the tests going?" Ray asked.

Scar bristled at the administrator's transparent attempt to divert attention from his misguided complaint. "Todd has an exemplary ability to concentrate, and a healthy respect for authority. That, however, does not stop him from exploring and trying to expand the limits of his personal power."

"Right." Ray shifted position, kicking a cat carrier on the floor by the desk. The animal inside hissed. "I finally caught that stray cat Hank let inside."

Ray had told Scar about the incident with Paige Matthews, the boy, and the cat. Ray had let Paige Matthews believe the creature was a pet, using the orange cat to plant false images in both their minds. As a result, the social worker thought Todd tormented animals, and Todd felt unjustly accused by someone he wanted to trust. In actuality, the boy hadn't mistreated the cat. The beast had eluded capture for days and wasn't about to let anyone grab it.

"It's outlived its usefulness," Scar observed.

"Chuck will take it to the pound later," Ray said.

"Why bother?" Scar was constantly amazed by the unnecessary complexity of twenty-first-century solutions to simple problems. "Just kill it or let it starve."

"An excellent suggestion." Ray nodded, but made no move to comply.

Irritated, Scar kicked the carrier and leaned over to open the wire door. He fully intended to end the hissing cat's life without further delay, but the phone rang. Modifying his voice to a slightly higher male register, he answered, "Yes?"

"Is this the South Bay clinic?" Todd asked.

Scar cast a sidelong glance at Ray and smiled. Although the man wasn't a bloodthirsty thug, his technical skill made up for it. Ray had rigged the Bay Haven phones so calls that were placed without the proper three-digit code were automatically routed to the office.

"Yes, this is South Bay Social Services," Scar continued in the male tenor. "How may I direct your call?"

"Paige Matthews, please," Todd asked. He sounded breathless. Whether from extreme stress or physical exertion Scar couldn't tell. Nevertheless, the boy's resourcefulness was admirable.

Scar pressed the hold button as Ray stepped over to the bank of surveillance equipment. "Todd is trying to reach the Matthews woman."

Ray keyed a control board and stepped back

as the picture on one of the monitor's shifted to
show Todd standing by a smaller office desk.
Ray pointed toward the closed door into the
adjoining office. "He's in there. Probably found
the number in the phone book."

This kid is just full of astounding surprises, Scar
thought as he reconnected with the boy's line. It
took a lot of nerve to place a forbidden phone
call right under the administrator's nose.

"Paige Matthews," Scar said, mimicking
Paige's voice.

"This is Todd, Todd Corman at Bay Haven."
The boy's tone was clipped, but anxious.
"You've got to get me out of here."

"I'm afraid that won't be possible, Todd." The
friendly lilt in Scar's Paige voice was replaced
with a hard, uncaring bite. "You should have
thought about the consequences before you
broke all your ties with the foster families.
There's nothing else I can do to help you now."

"But this Ray guy got us out of bed to run
laps in the middle of the night," Todd said with
a trace of desperation. "Then he made us take
cold showers in the basement!"

"Do you have permission to make this phone
call?" Scar as Paige asked.

"No, but Ray—"

"Listen to me, Todd, and listen good." Scar's
ability to replicate voices was the ideal means of
completely undermining Paige's position with
the boy. "Lying about Mr. Marino won't get you

anything but a quick trip to County Juvenile."

"I'm not—"

"I'm busy, Todd. Don't call me again." Scar hung up and glanced toward the closed door into the next room.

Todd's enraged scream reverberated throughout the lower level of the mansion. Before the high, piercing note died out, he was tearing the smaller office apart.

Scar watched the destruction on the surveillance monitor, marveling at the wrath in someone so young. When Ray took a step toward the door to intervene, Scar grabbed his arm.

"But he's wrecking the place," Ray protested. "He's got a long history of venting his anger on breakable objects."

"Doesn't matter," Scar said. "A Darklighter is being born."

A low guttural sound rumbled from Todd's throat as he pulled the phone cord out of the wall and heaved the multi-line device through a window. Teeth clenched and chest heaving, he ripped books off a bookcase and toppled the empty shelves. A lamp disintegrated into ceramic shards and twisted wires as he smashed it repeatedly against the desk. Nothing escaped the frenzied storm of the boy's hatred.

Scar had underestimated how much Todd had been poisoned by life. Whether his sense of abandonment and abuse was anchored in reality or existed only in his mind, the boy had steadily lost faith in everyone and everything. Now he believed Paige had turned against him too. It was just another reminder that nobody cared what became of him.

Scar nodded, pleased. Once the seeds of corruption took root in a human soul, the dark powers quickly supplanted all elements of good.

The boy ceased his rampage and stood glaring at the broken window. As his breathing calmed, the light in his eyes shifted from a bright boyish shine to a glint of absolute loathing.

Toward Paige or everyone? Scar wondered as the potential of the boy's abrupt shift in demeanor became clear.

Scar's original plan had involved cultivating boys and young men for Darklighter status upon their deaths as grown men. A more insidious concept occurred to Scar given the intensity of Todd's anger.

A *child* Darklighter would be an extraordinarily potent weapon against Whitelighters. Benign, naive, and easily misled by the appearance of innocence, a Whitelighter would let a kid get closer than caution dictated before it identified the young assassin as a Darklighter.

"Todd is ready to join us now," Scar said.

"He is with us." Ray frowned when he realized that Scar wasn't referring to the boy's residence at Bay haven. A look of horror crossed his gaunt face when he understood the true intent of the statement. "You mean Todd should become a Darklighter *now*?"

Scar nodded. "As soon as possible."

Ray paled, his voice cracking. "Wouldn't he have to die?"

"A mortal death only," Scar scoffed. "He'll be immortal when he awakens."

"But there's no guarantee Todd will meet the criteria to become a Darklighter, especially since he's so young."

Ray glanced at the monitor. Todd was no longer there, but the room looked as though a force five tornado had roared through. *No guarantee,* Scar thought, but he had given that problem much consideration. Since the Darklighter faction he envisioned depended on loyalty, those he chose had to be acceptable to the evil forces that granted position and power. He was confident he could convince boys like Todd to choose evil, but that was not necessarily enough to elevate them as Darklighters. There was, however, an elegant, albeit theoretical, solution.

Those Scar selected for his elite band of Darklighters might be able to prove themselves worthy of their eternal task by murdering innocents with Whitelighter qualities. With Todd as his first subject, he had hoped to prove or disprove the hypothesis.

Now, however, Scar had a unique opportunity to take the test a step further.

Although a human wasn't able to kill a Whitelighter, Todd could seize his destiny by killing someone with Whitelighter blood: Paige.

"Do you know where I left my wallet?" Cole paused by the dresser and patted his pocket.

"Let's see." Phoebe sat on the bed, propped against a mound of pillows. She closed her eyes and placed her fingertips on her temples. She frowned, feigning a deep concentration, then opened her eyes and asked, "Did you check the pants you wore yesterday?"

Cole's gaze darted to the pile of clothes he had dropped on the floor the night before. Phoebe had been in bed reading when he had finally gotten home from the university library. He had been so tired he had fallen asleep within seconds of his head hitting the pillow.

Phoebe arched an eyebrow when Cole picked up a pair of wrinkled trousers from the floor and pulled the wallet out of the back pocket.

His brow knit in playful consternation. "You think you're smart, don't you?"

"Absolutely," Phoebe teased back. "Too bad I can't make a career out of finding misplaced things left in obvious places."

"No luck at that temporary employment agency?" Cole pocketed the wallet and picked up his car keys.

"I'm lucky I left before I turned an extremely disagreeable man into a toad." Phoebe grinned.

"Not that Donald Ramsey doesn't deserve to live life as an amphibian, but toads have a bad enough rep already."

"I could stop by and punch his lights out on my way to the campus," Cole jokingly volunteered.

"Probably not a good idea." Phoebe sighed. "There's always a chance he'll get a client who wants a temp who's never had a real job and can't keep regular hours."

"Whatever you say." Cole leaned down to kiss Phoebe good-bye. "But if anything happens with the Darklighter, promise you'll call me."

"You're going back to the library, right?" Phoebe confirmed.

"Yes," Cole agreed. "I'll set my cell phone to vibrate so it doesn't disturb anyone."

"Okay." Phoebe drew her knees up and wrapped her arms around her legs. "Got time for coffee?"

"No, you let me sleep too late." Slinging a navy blue blazer over his shoulder, Cole waved and ducked out the door.

Phoebe threw on comfortable sweat pants, a T-shirt, and sneakers and went downstairs. With Paige at work, Piper and Leo shopping, and Cole on his way to the university, she was alone. The Manor felt forlorn and vacant.

The aura of loneliness struck Phoebe hardest in the kitchen, the hub of Halliwell morning activity. The coffeepot was empty, the dishes were done, and all evidence of last night's dinner had been cleared from the counters. However, something was cooling in a small caldron on the table near the cabinet that contained the herbs and potion ingredients.

Phoebe cast a curious glance at a half-cup of wet coffee grounds surrounded by bags and containers of other natural supplies. A sharp tang wafted from the dark liquid in the black pot. She wrinkled her nose and picked up a page torn from a spiral notebook. A recipe for growth compost was scrawled on the paper in Piper's handwriting.

"This could be interesting," Phoebe mumbled as she set the paper down. Although they couldn't use their powers for personal gain, Piper had dabbled in folk remedies as a hobby since their Halloween sojourn in the eighteenth century. Assuming the mixture was magical in origin and intended for plants, Piper's compost might produce some fascinating results.

Maybe a witch's batch of fantastic fertilizer was the inspiration for the "Jack and the Beanstalk" folktale, Phoebe thought, smiling. She grabbed a bottle of flavored iced tea from the refrigerator and took a PowerBar from a box in the pantry. With luck, the fumes from the growth compost pot would clear her head so she could compose a decent Darklighter vanquishing spell.

The light streaming in the window cast the attic in a magical glow that had a soothing effect on Phoebe's frayed nerves. Aside from her chronic state of unemployment, she knew that a demonic plot of Armageddon proportions often followed a prolonged period of no demon activity. Consequently the imminent Darklighter attack was a worry *and* a relief.

"And since relief is the better option, I should get busy and finish this spell." Phoebe set her drink on the table and flopped down in the rocker.

She retrieved her pad and pencil from the floor, unwrapped the PowerBar, and nibbled as she stared into space.

Nothing.

She shifted position, took another bite, placed the tip of the pencil on the paper, and wrote: *Dark enemy of White light in the fog . . .*

Having no clue where to go next, she doodled words that rhymed. *Flog, grog, log, hog, smog . . .* She stared at the list, drew a line through the whole lot, scribbled out

"fog," and replaced it with "mist."

"Much better." As Phoebe reached for the iced tea, her glance fell on the business card Paige had left on the table the night before. Wishing she could do something more for the lost boy, she picked up the card instead of the bottle.

The impact of the images that rushed into her head slammed her back in the rocker.

Phoebe saw Leo standing several feet from a

Darklighter, just as he had been in the previous vision. Now the thick fog dissipated into a fine, gray mist, allowing her to see the evil entity more clearly. A scar running from the bridge of his nose to below his left ear dominated a face that was a portrait of ruthless cruelty.

Black eyes seemed to hold Leo transfixed for a moment. Then the Darklighter's gaze and the angle of view shifted.

Phoebe snapped out of the trance gasping for air. Sweat beaded on her forehead. She didn't want to believe what the vision had revealed, but there was no mistaking what she had been shown.

Todd had raised a crossbow and fired a Darklighter arrow . . . at Leo.

Chapter
9

Paige Matthews's brush-off had left Todd feeling empty.

Except for the pain in the center of his chest.

With fifteen minutes of the break left, the classroom was empty. Todd slipped into his seat and dropped his head onto his arms.

The pain had started five years ago, when the hospital nurses put his mom on a rolling bed and pushed her through big double doors into the emergency room. He had been left alone in the waiting room. His neck had ached from watching boring news on a TV near the ceiling, but that was nothing compared to finding out he would never see his mother again. That pain, which had felt like a ball of hot metal at first, had dulled as time passed and had almost gone away.

It had come back last night, filling him with a

despair he thought he had conquered. Ray wasn't a pushover like the foster parents he had known. The administrator enjoyed making kids miserable. He had been determined to tough it out because he thought he had no choice.

Then, in the basement shower, he had remembered Paige.

Todd had been mad at the social worker for dumping him at Bay Haven until he recalled that Paige had also offered her card in case he needed anything. He had decided to call, hoping she would try to place him in another foster home, determined not to mess up again if she agreed.

Every social worker Todd had ever met had a soft heart, and he had honestly expected Paige to sympathize with his plight. He was still numb because she had refused to listen or help.

The shock had been so great and unexpected, he only had a vague recollection of what had happened after the phone went dead. He remembered broken glass and throwing things, but the daze hadn't passed until he had returned to the classroom.

Seized with the eerie feeling of being watched, Todd looked up.

Ray and the scarred test monitor were standing in front of his desk. They were both frowning.

Todd swallowed hard, bracing himself. Apparently Ray had found out that he had trashed the small office.

"We need to talk, Todd," Ray said evenly.

Scar sat down at the teacher's desk, preferring to let the administrator handle the confrontation.

Todd straightened up, meeting Ray's gaze.

The promise of a Whitelighter death, even that of the mongrel witch, had fueled Scar's impatience to press forward with the Darklighter project. The boy, with his cunning and instant grasp of the principles of power, would soon be a valuable tool in his arsenal.

"I'm listening." Todd folded his arms, a gesture of insolent defiance.

Scar nodded in silent approval. A touch of daring would help Todd through his imminent demise and, if all went well, his subsequent elevation. However, the boy still had to be primed to willingly relinquish his humanity with a murderous act.

"Paige Matthews just called, Todd," Ray said. "She's having you transferred to the County Juvenile Detention Center tomorrow morning."

The social worker hadn't called, of course. Like the intercepted phone call, Ray's announcement was a lie designed to drive Todd toward evil.

Todd absorbed the news with no outward sign that he was surprised or upset. "Did you ask her to do that?"

"Because you called her without permission and then destroyed the inner office?" Ray asked calmly.

"Yes." Todd answered flatly.

"No." Ray sighed, as though greatly disturbed. "Apparently Paige Matthews doesn't care as much about you as she wanted you to believe yesterday."

Todd just shrugged.

"That doesn't bother you?" Scar asked, indulging his curiosity. He planned to use Todd's sense of betrayal regarding Paige as the catalyst to turn the outraged boy into a killer.

"I'd rather stay here." The lack of emotion in Todd's voice suggested he honestly didn't care.

Has Todd already moved beyond needing vengeance as an excuse? Scar wondered, intrigued. It didn't matter whether the boy was hiding his feelings or if his insensitivity was more ingrained than Ray had anticipated. Both would work for Scar's purposes.

Phoebe paced the length of the garden plot. When she couldn't contact Leo and Piper or Paige after the second vision, she had gone outside to wait. Although cell phones helped them stay in touch most of the time, the compact devices didn't always work in remote areas or inside buildings.

They don't ring through when people turn them off, either, Phoebe thought. She had tried reaching Paige at the clinic, but her sister had an appointment in a client's home. Since interruptions could sour a meeting or inspection, Paige had her phone turned off.

Phoebe paused by a small table and two plastic chairs near the flowering shrubs. After checking her pocket for Paige's business card, she downed the rest of her iced tea.

"Where *are* they?" Phoebe pleaded with the cloudless blue sky.

"Who?" Piper's voice asked. "Us?"

Phoebe spun as Piper and Leo rounded the corner of the house. They each carried a flat of leafy plants into the backyard.

"Since when does it take hours to pick out tomato plants?" Phoebe demanded.

Leo looked at her askance. "Have you ever helped Piper pick out produce at the supermarket?"

"Oh. Enough said." Phoebe sighed. One secret of Piper's delicious gourmet cuisine was her insistence on using only the finest ingredients. As she liked to say in jest and often did, "The stew's only as good as what's in it."

When Leo set down the flat and left to get another, Phoebe gave the plants a closer look. "Well, they *are* perfect."

"They'd better be!" Blowing hair off her face, Piper planted her hands on her hips. "Five stores later."

"Perfect plants, a little magical growth compost—" Phoebe shot her sister a impish smile.

"Sounds like a garden any witch would be proud of."

"I certainly hope so." Piper grinned back, then frowned. "You're not waiting out here to pass muster on the pepper plants, Phoebe. What's going on?"

"You're cell phone's not," Phoebe said. "On, I mean."

"It's not?" Piper unclipped the phone and grimaced. "Oops. I forgot to charge the battery."

"You've got a few messages." Phoebe saw Leo returning and waited until he dropped another flat on the ground before she explained. "I had another vision, and since the fog was lifting, I'm pretty sure it qualifies as the second in a mist-and-stone series."

Leo stretched out on the grass, letting Piper and Phoebe have the plastic chairs. When Phoebe finished describing the vision she had gotten from the business card, she noticed that Leo seemed more perplexed than worried.

Piper was upset. "So what does that mean? That Todd is going to kill Leo instead of a Darklighter with a scar?"

"He can't," Leo said. "Todd is human."

"Not even with a Darklighter's crossbow?" Phoebe asked, recalling Natalie, the Whitelighter who had challenged Leo's methods of protecting his Charmed charges. "Eames was a warlock, and he killed Natalie."

"Eames killed a Darklighter, stole his crossbow, and absorbed the power to kill Whitelighters," Leo countered. "The presence of a mist means the events you saw are not set. Did you see the arrow hit? See me die?"

Phoebe shook her head.

"There you go." Leo shrugged it off.

"We've got to be missing something." Piper shuddered. "You met Todd, Phoebe. Has Paige totally misread him?"

"I don't think so, but I was only with him for a minute." Phoebe thought back to the brief encounter with the boy in Paige's cubicle. Todd had serious behavior problems, but he hadn't struck her as being evil. She couldn't bet Leo's life on a hunch, though. "It's possible," she conceded.

Piper shifted into take-charge mode. "If Todd isn't an innocent, we'd better find out and find out fast."

"Good idea, Piper." Leo stood up and brushed grass off his jeans. "We obviously missed something just popping in and out of Bay Haven, but a prolonged surveillance—"

"You're not going, Leo," Piper snapped. "We'll have to send Paige. She's not the target."

"She's visiting a client," Phoebe explained. "We won't be able to reach her until she leaves and turns on her-"

Phoebe was cut off by a loud woosh as the lawn suddenly burst into flames.

• • •

Concealed in the late afternoon shadow of the witches' Victorian house, Scar watched two of the legendary Charmed Ones respond to the fire he had ignited.

The Whitelighter grabbed Piper's wrist and orbed to safety in the ornamental garden.

Phoebe shot into the air, levitating out of harm's way. She cast a frantic look around, checking for witnesses as she hovered above the burning grass.

As Phoebe shifted her trajectory to land outside the ring of fire, Piper whirled. Her hands shot out in front of her, freezing the flames. Then she blew the top off a nearby sprinkler that was marked with red ribbon. Water spewed from the broken sprinkler head, dousing the flames when the fire roared back to life.

"What the hell just happened?" Piper stared at the blackened ground around the plot of tilled dirt.

"A close call with instant incineration," Phoebe said.

"Set off by the Darklighter or something else?" Piper cast a furtive glance around.

"Don't know," Phoebe said, "but if scorching the lawn is its best shot, I'm not terribly impressed."

You will be, Scar thought as he dissolved into a stream of black ash. He shimmered back into the cellar beneath the Bay Haven mansion and entered the dark passageway that led outside, confident the witches would respond as he anticipated.

As soon as Piper reached Paige by phone, the social worker would come to the home to check on Todd. Then, if Phoebe's vision was accurate, the Whitelighter would follow.

Playing right into my hands, Scar thought as he stepped into the courtyard. He was not concerned because the Charmed Ones could identify him or that the Whitelighter could destroy him. Leo wouldn't get the chance, and the witches' Power of Three would be neutralized.

Scar paused by a raised garden planter along the wall. The broad leaves of a dead plant crumbled when he touched it.

The perfect omen, Scar thought as the dark bits blew away on a light breeze. The Whitelighter and the witch would both die by Todd's hand—one before he transcended his mortal life, and one after.

Chapter
10

"No, I don't believe it." Paige's grip on the steering wheel tightened as she talked into her hands-free cell. Piper must have been redialing constantly to get through, because it had rung the second she'd turned it on. Now she understood the urgency. In Phoebe's latest vision, Todd had shot Leo with a Darklighter arrow.

"We don't want to believe it either," Piper said.

The sadness Paige detected in her sister's voice left no doubt about her sincerity. Leo was Piper's soul mate, and Phoebe's glimpses of the future were seldom wrong. Since that added up to Todd Corman, husband killer, Piper's concern for the boy was astonishing.

Except that Piper's a Charmed One, Paige thought. They were all still operating as though Todd was their innocent.

"Todd can't be evil," Paige said. "I'd know it."

"We have to know for sure, Paige," Piper insisted.

"You said Phoebe saw mist in this vision, too." Paige stopped talking to check an intersection for traffic before she whipped the VW around a corner. "That means what Phoebe saw isn't set in stone. Not yet."

"That's true, but—" Piper paused, then blurted, "There's something else."

Paige pulled the car to the curb, shifted into neutral, and stepped on the emergency brake. "What?"

"The lawn caught fire," Piper explained, rushing the words. "Under a clear blue sky for no reason. Woosh! The backyard was suddenly blazing."

"Two spontaneous combustion incidents can't possibly be a coincidence," Paige said evenly. Her heart thudded against her ribs and her pulse quickened for a moment as she settled into crisis calm. She had always had a capacity for keeping her head when things went critical.

"Probably not," Piper agreed, adding, "And although some high level demon totally unrelated to Todd or the visions might be responsible, that's not very likely either."

"Meaning the Darklighter Phoebe saw probably is," Paige finished. One of the oddities of their Charmed existence was the almost total absence of coincidence.

"That's our guess, Paige. If the Darklighter started the fire at the gas station, then chances are he saw you orb. If he did, he knows you're a Whitelighter too. At least, we have to assume he does."

"Right." Paige caught her lower lip in her teeth. The same thought had occurred to her. They weren't certain her Whitelighter ID had been blown, of course, but they had to proceed as though the worst had happened.

"Maybe you'd better come home," Piper said.

"Can't." Paige released the emergency brake and put the car in gear. "We have to know what's up with Todd. Since Leo's the target in the visions, I'm elected."

"But if you go to Bay Haven—" Piper's voice suddenly trailed off.

Phoebe came on the line. "The scenario in the vision isn't permanent yet, Paige. You're in danger too."

"I know that." Paige saw an opening in traffic and zipped back onto the street. "But if Todd is our innocent and he's with us at the Manor, the Darklighter can't use him as bait to lure Leo."

"Unless the Darklighter attack takes place here," Piper said in the background.

"It doesn't," Phoebe interjected. "I saw a high stone wall in the first vision, and we don't have one."

"I'm going to Bay Haven to get Todd out," Paige said. "I have to."

Phoebe didn't need further convincing. "Be careful."

When Phoebe disconnected, Paige speed-dialed the clinic to tell them she was on her way to the private home for a routine follow-up with Todd. She was going in the front door as the boy's caseworker, a cover she had inadvertently set up that morning. If Ray had discouraged her visit because he was genuinely concerned about Todd's adjustment, he'd be annoyed to see her, but compliant.

However, if she suspected the administrator was trying to isolate Todd for some other reason, she would orb the boy to safety without a second thought.

Phoebe stared at the phone after hanging up.

"Should we try to stop her?" Piper asked, reading the worry on Phoebe's face.

"No, we have to know if Todd is innocent." Phoebe pocketed her cell. She had a bad feeling too, but that wasn't unusual for a Charmed witch. "If Paige runs into trouble, she can orb."

Nodding, Piper turned in a circle scanning the yard. The burned strip of lawn paralleled the garden plot and measured roughly two feet by seven. The wet, charred grass matted under her shoes. "For the record, I blew up the sprinkler head on purpose."

"I think you made the right call." Phoebe surveyed the damage with a wry grin. Ironically

Piper was more relaxed and in control now that they had identified the threat.

Leo turned off the main valve to the sprinkler system and wiped his face with his shirttail as he walked back. "I can get a new sprinkler at the hardware store and replace the broken one in a few minutes. Not a big deal."

"Not for a handy man of your caliber." Piper frowned with another quick scan of the yard. "Any chance our supernatural arsonist is still here?"

"Doubt it." Leo squatted, holding his hand over a patch of scorched grass. His healing glow had no effect. "He saw you use your powers and tagged me as a Whitelighter. After that, he wouldn't have any reason to hang around."

"We're in the clear until sunset, though," Phoebe said. "It was still twilight in the second vision."

"So unless we hear from Paige sooner, we've got a couple of hours." Piper folded her arms and nodded. "Leo and I might as well put the time to good use and plant stuff."

"You plant." Leo retrieved the shovel he had left by the back door the previous day. He drove the spade into the ground and turned over a clump of scorched sod. "I'll bury the lawn."

"Well, there is a bright side." Piper answered Leo and Phoebe's questioning looks with a shrug. "We'll have a bigger garden."

"I'll go finish the spell." Phoebe ducked

inside before Piper thought to ask about her progress.

Armed with another iced tea, Phoebe hurried upstairs and closed the attic door. She hoped doing something to help vanquish the fire-setting Darklighter spy would soothe her jangled nerves.

"Here goes nothing." Sitting in the rocker, Phoebe set down the tea and stared at the memo pad. She had more to work with now that she had seen the Darklighter. His face was a blur except for the scar, but that might be enough. She read aloud the line she had already written, to test the feel of the spoken words.

"'Dark enemy of White Light in the mist—'"

Not bad, she thought as she scribbled the few rhyming words that came to mind. *Kiss, hiss, bliss, wrist, list, fist.* She tapped her chin with the pencil, paused, and wrote: a *mist, where death is written not in time or stone.* Phoebe straightened, pleased by the spurt of poetic insight.

"Two lines down and two to go, more or less." She smiled sadly for the phrases she so often had to cast aside. Until the whole incantation began to take shape, she had no idea if either line would survive as written.

The soft whirr of her cell phone ring broke the tranquil stillness. Phoebe fumbled the phone and hit send.

"Hello." A wide grin spread across her face. "Hi, Cole! How are the books treating you?"

"Where are you?" Cole sounded annoyed. "I tried the house phone, but no one picked up."

"I'm in the attic. Didn't hear it," Phoebe explained. "Piper and Leo are playing farmer in the yard, and Paige is off to Bay Haven to check on the kid."

"Are you busy?" Cole asked tentatively.

"Not too." Phoebe dropped the pencil and pad and picked up the iced tea. "Are you asking for a reason?"

"Yeah." Cole sighed. "I locked my keys in the car. Can you bring me the spare set? They're in the top drawer of the dresser."

Phoebe suppressed a startled laugh, amused because locking himself out of his car was such a human thing to do. "I would, but we don't have much time left before sunset, and I haven't finished the Power of Three spell."

"I left the library early to help. In case you hadn't noticed, I like Leo." Cole's tone was adamant. He was going to be part of the team no matter what. "Are you certain the twilight in your vision happens tonight?"

"Actually, no, I'm not." Phoebe stared at the pad. "It's just that without a spell—"

"I got passing grades in English poetry many decades ago," Cole quipped. "Bring me my keys, and I'll help you with it."

"Write a spell?" Phoebe hesitated. "Together?"

"I don't think making mystical words rhyme

is a life threatening activity." Cole sighed again, trying to quell his frustration. "Please, Phoebe. How many times has my knowledge of the dark realms helped since my demon half died?"

"Okay! You win." Phoebe flipped to a new page in the pad. "What parking lot, row, and space?"

After letting Piper and Leo know where she was going and why, Phoebe hit the San Francisco freeways. It had been so long since she had had to navigate rush-hour traffic, she had forgotten how maddening the ordeal could be. She kept her temper in check by composing the spell in her head. By the time she left the super highway and drove onto university property, the incantation was written in her mind.

Phoebe pulled over to write the spell in her memo pad before she forgot it. After the lines were committed to ink, she ripped the page off the pad, folded it, and put it in her pocket with Paige's business card. She was still wearing her casual clothes.

"That's okay," Phoebe muttered as she pulled back onto the road. "Cole loves my slightly scruffy, workout look."

Since she had attended the university the previous year, Phoebe knew her way around. She drove directly to the library parking lot and found Cole's row. However, someone else was parked in the numbered space he had told her.

Phoebe frowned. Had she written the number

down wrong? She had been concentrating so
hard on the spell she might have transposed the
double digit. She dialed Cole's cell as she began
a systematic search of the parking lot.

The bad feeling Phoebe had about Paige
going to Bay Haven alone intensified as she
drove up one row and down another. There was
no sign of Cole or his car, and he didn't answer
his cell phone. His voice mail didn't answer
either. After fifteen minutes, she parked to consider her options.

There's no way Cole got tired of waiting, Phoebe
thought. Cole was impatient and evasive on
occasion, but he was never inconsiderate of her
time or feelings. If something unforeseen had
forced him to leave the parking lot, he would
have called. He would not have left her stranded
or guessing what had happened to him.

So where is he and why didn't he call? Phoebe's
gaze snapped to the dashboard. She disconnected the cell phone from the hands-free unit.
On the off chance her speed-dial function wasn't
working, she punched in Cole's cell number. She
let it ring beyond the point his voice mail usually picked up.

There was no answer.

Nervous now, Phoebe dialed the house, Piper
and Paige's cell phones, and South Bay Social
Services. No one answered anywhere.

Phoebe placed the cell back in the hands-free
holder. For anyone else, a technological malfunc-

tion would be the logical explanation for a
phone going dead without warning. For a witch,
the reason was probably supernatural and sinis-
ter.

A magical entity could easily compromise
and use simple cell phone technology to place
false calls and interfere with real ones. All the
Halliwell phone numbers were a matter of public record.

And one of a Darklighter's most insidious tal-
ents was the ability to mimic voices.

So Cole probably didn't call at all! Phoebe realized as she peeled out of the parking space. She
tried not to panic as the most obvious implica-
tion of that assumption struck her.

The Darklighter had called pretending to be
Cole so he could separate her from her sisters.

A Power of Three spell was useless if the
Charmed Ones weren't together to recite it. *And
the best way to insure we can't possibly link up*,
Phoebe thought, *is to put us in three different loca-
tions.*

Paige's sense of foreboding had grown on the
drive along the remote county highway. As she
passed through the gateposts into Bay Haven, it
had become a huge, suffocating weight. She
could not escape the possibility that, in trying to
do what was best for Todd, she had delivered
him into the jaws of some monstrous evil.

Paige stopped her VW in the curved drive by

the front entrance and took a moment to compose herself. Without her sisters' powers as back up, she was easy prey. Her dread of the scarred Darklighter did not stem from cowardice, but from a grudging respect for her adversary.

Orbing was a great defense against a mortal such as Ray, but Darklighter's could shimmer, invade minds to implant suggestions, and impersonate voices. For her, the Whitelighter assassins were the embodiment of every scary thing she had ever imagined as a child.

Only this monster is under Todd's bed, too, Paige thought as she stepped out of the car and walked to the door.

She rang the bell and waited. When no one opened the door after a few seconds, she wiped a sweaty palm on her skirt and rang again. A minute then another passed with no response.

"Okay." Paige exhaled to quell a flutter of anxiety. Suddenly it seemed foolhardy to endanger her life and Todd's to protect a secret she might have to reveal anyway. What good could come of hiding her power if it killed her?

"There's an argument Piper can't win," Paige muttered. With her mind made up, she turned to go back down the steps. Deciding to orb Todd to safety and explain later was risky enough without turning into a beam of light in full view of anyone looking out the right window.

Paige had only taken a few steps when the door opened.

"Paige?"

Paige turned back at the sound of Ray's voice. He stood in the open doorway, frowning.

"Did I get our conversation wrong this morning?" Ray asked. "I thought we decided to put your visit off for a few days, until Todd started feeling comfortable here."

The administrator appeared puzzled, but Paige remained wary.

"Sorry, Ray, but my boss doesn't know the meaning of flexibility." Smiling, Paige shrugged as she headed back toward the door. "Stopping by to see Todd for a few minutes seemed easier than convincing Mr. Cowan to forego the normal routine."

"No rule is meant to be broken?" Ray asked as he stepped back to let her enter.

"Not for Mr. Cowan," Paige said. "Not broken, bent, or stretched."

Her joking manner was intended to throw Ray off guard. She wished she had decided to orb before she had announced her presence with the doorbell. Now that Ray knew she was there, it was too late to change course without arousing his suspicions. She could, however, do exactly what she had just told him she would: Check in and out with Todd as quickly as possible. Then, after she had driven a safe distance away, she could orb back to whisk the boy out.

As Ray closed the door, Paige's attention was drawn to a pathetic mewing sound. A cat carrier sat on the floor by the stairs. The plastic container was full of orange fur.

"Is something wrong with Hadie?" Paige asked, assuming the cat had been confined for a trip to the vet.

"Nothing that a blow to the head won't solve," Ray said.

Paige was blindsided by the conversational tone that momentarily masked Ray's actual words. When the awful truth dawned on her a fraction of a second later, she started to orb. She barely glimpsed the cruel intent etched on Ray's lean face or the police baton he wielded with brutal force.

When the hard rubber bat hit, a stabbing pain and a flash of gray exploded in her skull.

The instant Phoebe suspected a Darklighter plot to negate the Power of Three, she knew she had to connect with her sisters.

Focused on the problem and not the road, Phoebe almost missed the exit. She swerved into the far right lane, sped down the ramp, and slammed on the brakes at a stop sign. Turning right onto a two-lane highway, she stomped on the gas. Her mind raced as she roared past two mini-mart gas stations, a motel, and a fast-food restaurant.

The moment Piper had mentioned the possibility of an attack at the Halliwell house, Phoebe had remembered that the manor was not the location in her visions. Since Todd was irrevocably involved, logic strongly suggested that the confrontation would take place at the stone mansion.

That's where Paige had gone. That's where she was going. And Piper would be there too.

The outcome of the events depicted in her mist-and-stone visions might still be undetermined, but certain elements were set. Leo *would* go to Bay Haven, and if Leo went, Piper would not be left behind. The forces of universal magic bound the Charmed Ones as surely as the laws of physics held the subatomic particles of an atom in place.

The Power of Three was not easily voided.

That, however, did not necessarily mean they could thwart the Darklighter's plans.

Plans for what exactly? Phoebe wondered. Why had she seen *Todd* fire the crossbow at Leo and not the Darklighter?

As important as Leo was to all the Halliwell women, Phoebe sensed that the Whitelighter was a pawn in whatever the scarred creature hoped to accomplish.

Phoebe accelerated, as though exceeding the speed limit would help her think. Just before the backyard had turned into a blazing inferno, she had been on the verge of remembering an exchange she and Paige had had the night before. It suddenly surfaced now, an important piece of the unfolding situation.

" . . . there's something in everyone's life that can push them over the edge, to a point of no return," Phoebe had said.

Paige had nodded. "For Todd, that something might be our mysterious Darklighter."

Paige's words supported the idea that Todd might not be just a bystander when the Darklighter attacked. Maybe he was the key to the Darklighter's ultimate goal.

Which is? Phoebe frowned, sorting through everything she knew about Darklighters, looking for any tidbits of info that might solve the puzzle.

Although all Darklighters existed to kill Whitelighters, they often attacked the problem from different angles.

The Darklighter Alec had an enhanced command of heat, which he had used to burn his victims to a crisp. Before he had been vanquished by his own power, he had tried to procreate evil by mating with Daisy, an innocent under Leo's protection.

Phoebe frowned as she cruised the winding country highway as fast as she dared. Nothing about Alec seemed relevant to Todd's situation.

The warlock Leo had mentioned in the yard had killed a Darklighter with an athame to gain its killing power. Eames's plan to leave all good witches unprotected by eliminating all Whitelighters was brilliant, but doomed once the Charmed Ones had unraveled the scheme.

But we're not dealing with a warlock, Phoebe thought. The scarred personage she had seen in the second vision was definitely a Darklighter.

Maggie Murphy had almost committed suicide because a Darklighter convinced her that she brought bad luck to those she tried to help. He had tried to prevent her from becoming a Whitelighter to begin with.

Phoebe's frown deepened. People who lived pure, selfless lives, such as Maggie and Leo, became Whitelighters after they died. That begged the question: Did extremely bad people become Darklighters?

Yes! Phoebe thought, excited. Something Leo had said supported that conclusion: "Darklighters fill their ranks from the bad just as Whitelighters are recruited from the good."

Todd's situation fit those parameters.

At age twelve, Todd was an incorrigible troublemaker who didn't seem to care about anyone or anything. He had been sent to Bay Haven, a private home for delinquent boys, which wasn't subject to the strict oversight of a government facility. If Ray Marino had been bribed or otherwise enlisted into the Darklighter's service, there was no better place to find likely Darklighter material.

The car skidded around a curve when Phoebe pressed down on the gas. She couldn't prove her theory until she got to Bay Haven, but she was certain her deductions were correct.

The scar-faced Darklighter was using the home as a source of troubled boys he could turn into future Darklighters.

Or is he planning something worse than that? Phoebe gasped, remembering the image of Todd with the crossbow.

The boy *could* kill Leo if he had already become a Darklighter!

Neither she nor her sisters had considered that possibility, because the thought of anyone deliberately killing Todd to create a child Darklighter was too horrendous. But nothing else explained what she had seen in the second vision.

"Leo!" Phoebe called out, sending an urgent summons through the mystic channels that connected Whitelighters with witches. "Leo, it's important!"

As the seconds ticked by and Leo didn't respond, Phoebe assumed that something more imperative than his own safety had come up.

Like Paige? Phoebe wondered.

Paige had gone to Bay Haven to rescue Todd without a clue that the boy may have already become a Whitelighter assassin. If Leo sensed that she was in danger, he would go to Bay Haven to help her.

Phoebe fervently hoped that Piper had gone with him. The Power of Three spell might be Leo's only defense against the scarred Darklighter.

To assure herself that all was not lost, Phoebe reached for the folded incantation. Her fingers touched the business card she had put in her pocket after the second vision.

A third vision snagged her consciousness with such force, the car careened off the road toward a tree-lined ditch.

Chapter

11

When Paige first came to, she was aware of two things: the throbbing ache in her head where Ray's baton had struck and the hard surface beneath her. She stayed still with her eyes closed, trying to orient herself without alerting Ray that she had regained consciousness.

The only sounds were the slow drip of water into a pool and the gentle rustle of dry leaves in a light breeze.

Her nostrils flared with the musky scent of damp decay and dirt.

The rough surface under her hand and cheek felt like flat stone coated with moisture and patches of soft moss.

Sensing nothing else, Paige opened her eyes. It was immediately evident that she was lying in the stone courtyard. The diagram Leo had seen placed it behind the Bay Haven mansion set into the sloping terrain. Through an archway built into the high stone walls, she gazed at an expanse of green lawn and meadow. The sun had just begun to dip behind the trees in a distant wood.

Dusk, Paige thought, *but no fog.* If this was the reality symbolized in Phoebe's visions, she couldn't tell if events were finally set in stone or still subject to change. Leo wasn't present, which suggested the latter.

One aspect of her situation was clear, however. She had no reason to hang around waiting for Ray to return.

Except that she couldn't move.

Paige grunted, trying but unable to raise her head or hand. She closed her eyes to orb, but the power that flowed through her veins like warm butter just before her cells shifted from solid to light was inert. Before this frightening fact could register, someone twined fingers in her hair and yanked her onto her knees.

"Going somewhere?" A scarred man asked. He was dressed in the black garb of a Darklighter: black turtleneck, jacket, and trousers. The harsh, gravelly sound of his voice burrowed into the ear like bore worms into wood.

Seized with the cold terror of total helplessness, Paige stared into eyes that were too black to reflect light.

Sensing her fear, the Darklighter's lip curled into a crude facsimile of a smile.

Born with a stubborn streak that had driven her parents and teachers crazy, Paige glared back. She might be helpless, but if she was going to die, she was going out with her pride and self-respect intact.

"You should be very afraid, Paige." The Darklighter glanced to the side. "Right, Todd?"

"Yes, Scar."

Paige's throat constricted when Todd stepped into view. The boy met her stare in sullen silence, conveying the same venom toward her that she felt toward the Darklighter.

"Make no mistake, Paige," Scar said. "You are helpless."

The statement was intended to heighten Paige's despair. She couldn't help being overcome by futility, but it wasn't caused by the Darklighter's physical power over her. It came from the complete absence of emotion on Todd's young face.

Without warning, Scar pushed Paige onto her side and dragged her to the base of a stone planter. She collapsed like a rag doll when he let go of her hair, and she couldn't resist when he lifted her under the arms and propped her against the stone. Her head drooped, making it difficult to follow the Darklighter's movements.

"Are you wondering *why* you can't move?" Scar stooped down to look Paige in the eye. When she wouldn't look away, he smiled as though her defiance was a victory for him.

Todd hung back, glaring at Paige.

"I was born in the first century," Scar said. "Yes, you heard that right. The *first* century."

Todd shifted his gaze to the Darklighter, obviously surprised by this revelation.

"I was an undefeated gladiator, a free man of Rome who gloried in death and packed the Colosseum." Scar paused to smile ruefully. "Of course, many of those spectators came hoping to see me die. Eventually I did, but that was just the beginning of another, greater existence."

Paige could care less about the Darklighter's ghastly history. However, the longer he talked, the better her chances of survival. Piper and Phoebe would mount a rescue when she didn't answer her phone or check in.

"Those were dark, powerful times," Scar went on. "The underworld roiled with a ferocity never known in the mortal realm, not among the most primitive tribes or in Rome's great arena. The secrets of the primordial black arts had not yet been lost when I awakened."

"What secrets?" Todd asked.

"For one, a potion that inhibits a Whitelighter's power to move or orb." Scar kept his eye on Paige as he spoke and pulled a small glass vial from the pocket of his black jacket. "It's made of some exquisitely rare and expensive ingredients, but then, it's very effective, isn't it?"

Paige would not have honored the question

with an answer if she had been able to speak. It was depressing to see Todd absorbing Scar's every word. She could sense the boy embracing the temptations the Darklighter dangled in front of his young, susceptible mind.

"Don't tell anyone," Scar chided as though taking her into his confidence, "but I'm the only Darklighter left who knows how to mix it. That's a temporary situation, however."

The enormity of his words sent an electric jolt to Paige's heart. A potion that rendered Whitelighters immobile and helpless would allow a heavily armed Darklighter to wipe out several of the guardians with impunity.

"Most of my kind are too proud or thrilled by the hunt to use an inhibitor." Scar scoffed, shaking his head. "The fools act as though goodness and Whitelighters are a finite commodity that can be eradicated."

Without Whitelighters to kill, what would Darklighters do? Paige wondered, but Scar's next revelation made the question a moot point.

"Unfortunately some of the necessary ingredients, which I have hoarded over the years, are extracted from extinct species." Scar motioned Todd closer and placed a hand on the boy's shoulder.

Paige studied the boy, noting a scratch on his cheek and a dull purplish bruise on his arm. He was alive.

"But the potion won't be lost. It's only one of

many ancient arts I intend to pass on to my protégé." Scar bent over to glare at Paige. "But *that*
secret will die with you."

Todd showed no sign of caring one way or
the other, but Paige could not believe he was a
cold-blooded killer. If she had so drastically mis-
judged him, she could not trust her instincts
about other kids in the future.

If I have a future, she thought wryly.

Scar held up his arm, and a crossbow
appeared in his hand. Black poison clung to the
sharpened tip of the loaded arrow. He handed
the weapon to Todd.

Paige wasn't sure if she saw a flicker of doubt
in Todd's eyes or if it was a manifestation of
wishful thinking. He took the crossbow, but did
not raise it.

"She came to take you to County Juvenile,
Todd," Scar said evenly. "You know what that
means."

What? Paige stared at Todd, hoping to com-
municate her frantic denial with her eyes. Scar
was lying, but the boy had no way of knowing
that.

"Six years of misery before the child welfare
system releases you when you turn eighteen."
Scar sighed. "Six years of bad food, hard labor,
and homework, no perks, and then you'll be
tossed out with nothing. That's the future Paige
wants for you."

Paige tried to shake her head, but nothing hap-

pened. She had not arranged to have the boy transferred, but Scar's description of life at the county
facility gave the accusation an aura of truth. The
Darklighter's words painted a darker picture, but
they were eerily similar to what she had told the
boy about County Juvenile the day before.

"If you survive that long," Scar added. "Paige
doesn't care if you live or die, Todd. Not like Ray
and I care."

Paige's pulse and respiration rates increased
despite the effects of Scar's potion. None of the
ugly, murderous demonic powers she had
encountered since becoming a Charmed One
had filled her with as much trepidation as the
festering hatred in Todd's brown gaze.

Tears for the lost boy misted her eyes. Todd
was just a kid, an adolescent caught between the
heartaches of a tragic childhood and the unforgiving realities he envisioned for tomorrow.
With no one but the traitorous administrator and
the lying Darklighter to influence him, the boy
had no genuine guidance.

"You'd be better off at Bay Haven, Todd,"
Scar said, "but you can't stay here unless Paige is
gone."

Paige stared at the boy as he raised the crossbow.

"Kill her, Todd," Scar pressed. "It's the only
way."

The boy's hands flexed on the weapon as he
sighted down the arrow shaft.

Paige tensed. The Darklighter poison was fatal.

"Uh-oh."

Piper stopped patting dirt around the roots of a pepper plant when Leo stopped digging and stiffened. "What?"

"It's Paige." Leo dropped the shovel. "She's in major trouble."

"What's wrong?" Piper jumped up and pulled off her garden gloves. She thought about the scarred Darklighter as she looked toward the western sky. The sun had just dipped below the neighborhood roof-line.

"I'm not sure," Leo said, "but her terror is so great I can feel it."

"It's got to be the Darklighter, Leo." Piper stared at the ground. She had sensed Paige's fear whenever the subject of the Darklighter had come up, but she couldn't fault her half sister's worry. With all the mortal threats the Charmed Ones faced, she and Phoebe didn't have Whitelighter blood or the added burden of being Darklighter prey.

"She's either cornered or captured—" Leo gasped.

"Please, no. . . ." Piper covered her mouth with her hand, assuming the worst: Leo had just felt Paige die.

"Paige?" She asked softly.

Leo shook his head. "Phoebe, but—she's gone."

"Gone?" Piper paled. "What does that mean?"

"I got a flash of something. Panic, maybe?" Leo exhaled, shaking his head in frustration. "I'm not sure what because it happened so fast. I was connected with Phoebe for an instant and then—nothing."

Piper's throat went dry, and she fought back a rush of tears.

"Phoebe's off my radar, Piper." Leo touched Piper's cheek. "Can you try to find her while I go help Paige?"

Piper understood why he couldn't ignore Paige's plight. She couldn't stand by doing nothing either, not while her husband and sisters' lives were in jeopardy.

The Power of Three spell would remove the Darklighter threat, but they didn't know where Phoebe was, how she was, or if she had finished writing the incantation. Besides, unless the Charmed Ones were together, the spell was worthless.

"If the Darklighter has Paige," Piper said, "you'll be orbing right into a trap."

"I don't have any choice." Leo pulled his hand free.

"I know, but I have an idea." Piper sighed. "It's risky and might not work, but it's the best I can do with only a few seconds to plan."

"Talk fast," Leo said.

• • •

Phoebe woke up with a moan, her head resting on the steering wheel. For a few seconds, she couldn't remember where she was or what had happened. She touched her forehead as she sat up, then gawked at the blood on her fingers.

She blinked with surprise at the open wound and to clear her blurred vision. A folded paper and business card lay in her lap, and the windshield was cracked. The steam rising from under the hood jogged her memory.

Fog!

"Oh, boy." Phoebe inhaled sharply as events of the past several minutes came flooding back. She had driven off the road when Paige's business card set off another vision.

A rush of adrenalin spurred Phoebe to instant action. The car could catch fire, and she had to get out. She pulled on the door handle, but the door wouldn't open. The impact with a sizeable tree had buckled the metal around the hinges.

"Stay calm and think." Phoebe took a deep breath and noticed that the ignition key was still turned on.

She pushed the button for the power window on the driver's side. The small motor whirred, but the crunched metal frame jammed the glass.

Other side! She frantically depressed the button for the passenger side window. When that didn't open, she unbuckled her seat belt, grabbed the spell paper off her lap and the cell phone off the dashboard, and tumbled into the

back seat. The back door opened without diffi-
culty, and she tumbled out of the car into tall
grass.

The long hours of Cole's coaching in the art of
survival came to Phoebe's aid now. She immediately rolled clear of the crashed vehicle, jumped
to her feet, and moved off to a safe distance.
Exhaling with relief, she wiped a trickle of blood
from the corner of her eye and surveyed the
damage.

Although she had just totaled her car, the
accident could have been a lot worse. When she
had gone into the vision trance, the car had
swerved off the highway by a grassy slope. The
upward incline had slowed the car's forward
motion before it rammed the tree, saving her
from serious injury.

Or worse, Phoebe realized with a shudder.
Since she had only suffered bumps, bruises, and
a large cut, she quickly shifted mental gears.

The third mist-and-stone vision had been
awash in death, just not hers.

Phoebe swayed on her feet, suddenly dizzy
from the blow to her head. She sank to her knees
and doubled over with nausea. Closing her eyes,
she willed the physical symptoms of a delayed
stress reaction to pass as the horrifying vision
replayed in her mind.

*Wisps of mist drift across damp, moss covered
stones, like ghosts mocking the fading fog. . . . The
glint of defiance in Paige's eyes as a Darklighter*

arrow pierces her heart, death instant and not a lingering agony . . . flesh melting off bone as a phantom Todd emerges from skeletal remains, raises the crossbow with a black hand, and fires . . . at Leo. . . .

Phoebe gagged, wishing she could erase the terrible images. If the vision came to pass, Todd would kill Paige, the scarred Darklighter would kill the boy, and he would transform into a teenaged Darklighter and kill Leo. The presence of the symbolic mist meant that the outcome could still be changed, but time was running out.

Stumbling to her feet, Phoebe clutched the Power of Three spell in her fist and glanced at the two-lane highway. No car or truck had passed since she had awakened. In fact the road had been practically deserted before she had crashed.

Steam still hissed from the damaged radiator. The car wasn't going anywhere.

Phoebe tried to dial Piper's cell, but her digital screen didn't light up. Either the phone had been damaged in the crash, the battery had gone dead, or the Darklighter's magical interference was still in effect. She tossed it on the ground by the car to retrieve later.

"Leo!" Desperate, Phoebe scrambled up the incline toward the woods as she cried out to the Whitelighter. When he hadn't appeared by the time she reached the trees, she was certain he wasn't coming.

Because he's dead or because he's too busy trying to save Paige?

The answers to all her questions waited at Bay Haven a few miles down the road. She just had to get there.

Hitchhiking wouldn't cut it. There wasn't enough traffic. Besides, dressed in scruffy sweats with a huge gash on her face, she looked like a refugee from a disaster movie. Anyone who stopped to offer her a ride would want to take her to the nearest emergency room.

"How far am I from Bay Haven anyway?" Phoebe muttered as she pushed into the thick stand of trees. When she was well beyond sight of the highway, she clamped the folded paper in her teeth, and slowly rose into the air to get her bearings.

The empty highway curved to the left then straightened for the final stretch to the stone mansion. Phoebe estimated the distance at a mile if she followed the road, a half mile as the crow flies.

Or the witch runs, Phoebe thought as she settled back to the ground and headed through the forest on foot.

Paige stared down the shaft of the Darklighter arrow, counting down the seconds. She had been in some tough spots before, but there was an unnerving certainty about her circumstances now. Her calm in the face of imminent death surprised her. Her worst fears were coming true, but her resolve was unshaken. The Darklighter's terrifying presence and manipulative comments could not break her spirit.

"Prolong the moment, Todd," Scar said. "Savor the fear you see in her eyes. Make her suffer."

Scar's husky voice seemed to have a hypnotic effect on the boy. Todd swayed slightly, watching her, letting himself be coaxed into doing Scar's bidding.

In a moment of clarity, Paige suddenly realized that Scar did not want Todd to shoot—not just yet.

Why not? Paige wondered. The reprieve was only momentary at best, but her relief was profound. Every second bought precious time that could mean the difference between living and dying. *For me, but what about Leo?*

Leo was the reason she was still alive.

Paige mentally kicked herself. That conclusion seemed obvious now that it had occurred to her.

The Darklighter was using her as bait to lure the Whitelighter, a ploy that wouldn't work if Leo knew that she was dead. In fact Scar's macabre taunts were designed to augment her fear so Leo couldn't help but sense it.

So much for trying to cut out the designated protector, Paige thought. However, since the Whitelighter posse of one hadn't orbed in to save her, she might still be able to save him. *By thinking happy thoughts?*

"See that?" Scar spoke to Todd, pointing toward Paige. "Her eyes burn with the desire to live and the false hope our hesitation has given her. Should we continue the torment or end her misery?"

Oops, Paige thought, wincing. Maybe Leo wasn't the target after all. She certainly hadn't intended to give her captor any ideas.

Surprised by the unexpected ability to move, Paige froze. A flinch wasn't much, but it indicated that Scar's inhibitor potion was wearing off. Perhaps the ancient immobilizing agent was only partially effective on a half-Whitelighter.

The Darklighter's attention was on the boy and he hadn't noticed the telltale facial tick.

"Let's wait," Todd said. His body was as rigid as the one-eyed stare he kept trained on Paige.

"Yes, let's wait." Suddenly annoyed, Scar scanned the courtyard.

He's looking for Leo, Paige deduced. Considering how terrified she was, the Whitelighter's absence was puzzling.

But then, considering Todd's nervous grip on the deadly crossbow, it was just as well Leo hadn't materialized out of thin air. If the boy had never seen Scar shimmer, seeing someone orb might startle him into pulling the trigger.

Orbing, however, was the only realistic option she had, provided she regained more freedom of movement before Scar decided she had outlived her usefulness.

As Scar's glance swept over her face, Paige kept

her expression neutral. Any chance to escape would evaporate if the killer suspected his potion wasn't working as well as he thought. She breathed easier as his gaze continued on around the stone enclosure, but she sensed that his patience and her reprieve were both about to expire.

She would only get one attempt to orb. If she failed, she was dead.

Paige's left hand had gotten tucked partially underneath her when Scar had rudely raised her into a sitting position against the wall. Now, without letting the effort show on her face, she tried to move it.

Her fingers jumped.

Every muscle in Paige's body tensed as she tried to still her shaking hand. The effects of the potion were wearing off at a faster rate than she had realized.

It's now or never, Paige decided when Scar suddenly looked back. Mustering every ounce of strength and concentration she possessed, she willed her physical body into transition.

As Paige began to orb out, Todd looked up from the crossbow, his eyes wide.

"Shoot her!" Scar commanded.

Too late, Scar. Paige would have gloated as she slipped from the Darklighter's grasp, but the last thing she saw before the courtyard faded was Leo and Piper orbing in.

Chapter
12

Phoebe summoned a burst of speed when she saw the Bay Haven mansion through the trees. Staying far from the highway, she had made excellent time navigating through the dense forest.

Pausing in the shade of a large oak, Phoebe scouted the area she had to cross to reach the house. There were only a few trees for cover on the lawn between the woods and the mansion. She tracked the rumbling sound of a motor to the dim headlights of a tractor mowing a meadow beyond the landscaped lawns that surrounded the mansion. The driver was probably Herman, the home's gardener and maintenance man.

In the waning daylight, she could see the man hunched over the steering wheel, his attention on the tall weeds that fell beneath the mower blades. The tractor made a hard right turn and headed down an incline. The tension drained

from Phoebe's arm and leg muscles as the tractor vanished from sight.

Once again, the basement training sessions
with Cole would serve her well. Her stamina
and speed had dramatically improved over the
past weeks. As long as the tractor didn't make a
sudden U-turn and no one looked out the windows during the next couple of minutes, she
could sprint the distance without being seen.

Breathing in deeply, Phoebe tightened her
grip on the spell. She broke from hiding in the
trees at a full run and pounded across the closely
cropped grass. Her sneakers thudded the
ground in a steady, staccato rhythm that helped
her maintain the blistering pace.

As Phoebe closed the gap, she imagined Cole
looking up from his law texts to cheer her on.
When she had figured out that the cell phones
weren't working, she had been so worried about
Paige and Leo, she had assumed Cole was still
hitting the books in the university library. As she
raced across the immaculate lawns, she suddenly wondered if the Darklighter had just gar-
bled the phone call from Cole. What if he was
waiting for her in a *different* parking lot?

Then he's totally upset and angry, but safe,
Phoebe thought. She put Cole out of her mind
when the bluish-white light of an orb appeared
in the driveway just ahead.

Paige materialized in a sprawled position on
the pavement. The instant she finished forming,

she scrambled to her feet and staggered to the edge of the driveway.

Phoebe altered the angle of her run to intercept. Whatever Paige had been through before she had orbed, it had left her weak and disoriented.

"Phoebe!" A strained smile lit Paige's face as Phoebe skidded to a halt in front of her.

"It's too open here, Paige." Phoebe waved toward the end of the house as she took Paige's arm and urged her to move. "Come on."

Supporting Paige, Phoebe eased between the low branches of two spreading juniper shrubs. They both sat, hidden from view by the bushes, hugging the wall.

"What happened to you?" Phoebe asked.

Paige flicked a finger for each item she rattled off. "Knocked out by Ray, immobilized by Scar's ancient potion, and almost killed by Todd."

"So the vision was right!" Phoebe exclaimed.

"No." Paige waved her hands in a negative motion. "Todd was going to kill *me*, not Leo."

"I had a third vision," Phoebe said. "Todd kills you. Scar kills Todd. Todd becomes Darklighter and then he kills Leo."

"Oh." Paige scowled, thinking. "Was there a mist?"

Phoebe nodded. "Yeah, and the fact that you orbed out alive is proof that it wasn't set in stone. Whatever's going on now, though—I haven't seen it."

"Scar is what's going on now." Paige's eyes flashed with indignation. "He wants to turn Todd to evil, and I don't know if it's too late to stop him."

"If we had three Charmed witches"—Phoebe held up the folded paper—"I've got a Power of Three spell to vanquish a Darklighter with a scar."

Paige smiled and grabbed Phoebe's arm. "Well, I've got the third witch."

No matter how often Phoebe orbed as a passenger on Paige or Leo's photon express, the experience was never routine. She was always stricken with a twinge of fear when her mind brushed the infinite vastness of the cosmos and filled with relief when she coalesced into solid form again. Also, as usual when emergency circumstances forced her to orb, she didn't have time to dwell on the disquieting effects.

Phoebe and Paige materialized in a stone courtyard as the sun disappeared from the sky. Late afternoon shadows melded with a twilight gloom enhanced by dead plants, damp stones, and broken statues.

There was no mist, real or symbolic.

Phoebe was glad she hadn't had a fourth and final vision that revealed how events would play out. Her normal visions were windows on futures that might happen if she and her sisters didn't act to change them. The immutable certainty of the mist-and-stone effect denied the ability to make a difference. Now, because Phoebe didn't know what fate had in store, she would act on instinct without prejudice.

Just as Phoebe and Paige appeared, Piper threw a freeze whammy on Todd, who was about to fire the crossbow at Leo.

"A couple of minutes ago Todd was aiming that thing at me," Paige muttered.

Close call, Phoebe thought as she took in the whole scene.

She and Paige were standing by a raised stone garden area full of dead, brown plants. Piper and Leo stood twenty feet away, facing them. The boy had almost completed an about face pivot, as though Leo and Piper's entrance from behind had caught him by surprise. Piper's flash freeze had rendered him and the Darklighter crossbow harmless for the moment.

The Darklighter stood ten feet to the side on Phoebe's right, between the witches. Tall with a sinewy, muscular build, he was unaffected by Piper's magic.

"Where have you two been?" Piper asked, cocking an eyebrow.

"Just comparing notes in the driveway," Paige quipped.

"How dare you make jokes in my presence!" Scar's black eyes gleamed with outrage. The air around him seemed to quiver with the force of his fury and power.

"Jokes? Like keeping Todd from ruining his

afterlife?" Phoebe met the Darklighter's challenging glare without flinching. "Sorry about that."

"No, she's not," Piper clarified.

Phoebe wondered how long they could keep the Darklighter talking. Since his plan to prod Todd into committing murder had been foiled, Scar had no reason to stick around. He could shimmer back to the underworld to fall back, regroup, and strike again, unless the Charmed Ones hit him with the Power of Three spell first. To do that, they had to read the spell in unison, and Piper was on the opposite side of the courtyard.

Phoebe unobtrusively tugged Paige's blouse as she took a step toward Todd. Paige gave her a subtle nod, indicating she understood that they both had to join Piper. Adopting a worried posture, Paige gave an appearance of aimless wandering as she moved along the outer wall.

Phoebe had the Darklighter's attention as she took another step toward Todd. She wanted him to think she was flaunting misguided confidence with a close inspection of the frozen boy.

"Actually I'm not sorry at all." As Phoebe came abreast of Todd, she cast a quick, questioning look at the Darklighter.

"Scar," Paige said as she ambled toward Piper along the wall. "He calls himself Scar."

"Who would have guessed?" Piper quipped.

The Darklighter's incensed reaction to their

glib disrespect had provided a psychological opening. Phoebe plowed into it with an even more pointed, impertinent attitude.

"Whatever," Phoebe said, dismissing Scar's identity with a wave. She was gambling that, in his arrogance, the Darklighter would insist on having the last word. "You can't hurt us."

Todd unfroze at that moment. In the instant before Piper froze him again, his finger pulled the trigger back. The next time he started to move, the arrow would fly.

"Can't I?" Scar sneered with a triumphant look at Todd.

Despite her concern for Paige and Leo, Phoebe had not forgotten their primary mission to save innocents. Until Todd completed an irrevocable act of evil, he was not beyond saving.

"You aren't getting this kid," Phoebe said. "You lose."

"Fool," Scar scoffed. "I have already beaten you."

"How do you figure that?" Leo asked.

Phoebe glared at the Darklighter as she inched forward. Paige had stopped within two strides of Piper's position.

"When that immobilizing power wears off, Todd's arrow will fly, and his fate will be sealed." Scar spoke with unguarded disdain, as though addressing mental morons.

Phoebe was not insulted. His sense of superiority and invincibility against mere witches would contribute to his undoing.

Phoebe forced herself to keep her movements unhurried. If Scar realized the Power of Three was coming together before the Charmed Ones could act, he could escape with ease.

"Blackening the boy's soul beyond redemption will not require much work," Scar concluded. "Todd is mine when he dies. As a child or an adult, I do not care."

Phoebe's own outrage erupted as she moved into place beside Piper. She could make darn certain that Scar had "adopted" his last young victim.

Let's see if you care about this, Phoebe thought. As Scar began to shimmer, she started to recite the Power of Three incantation.

"'Dark enemy of White light . . .'"

Black ash flaked off the Darklighter's contours as Piper and Paige added their voices to Phoebe's.

"'. . . in a mist, where death is written not in time or stone. . . .'"

Phoebe's heart fluttered as the words arrested the Darklighter's attempt to shimmer. His body convulsed as he was seized by the potent spell.

"'. . . but in the fire cast by demon fist; burn Dark light shadow, scar and blood and bone.'"

Phoebe and her sisters tensed as they chanted the final phrase. They watched, silent and still, as the Darklighter was consumed in an agony of fire and black smoke. No one stirred for a moment after the last flame flared and died.

"Todd!" Paige turned toward the boy.

Phoebe followed her sister's gaze. A look of utter contempt twisted the boy's face. The weapon was still primed to fire when he resumed moving.

"It's hard to believe Todd's a killer." Piper pulled Leo to the side and stepped in front of him as an extra measure of protection. The Darklighter arrow could inflict a mortal wound if her freeze power didn't stop it, but the poison wouldn't kill her.

"He's not." Paige's expression revealed a deep anguish. "He can't be."

Phoebe realized that Paige wasn't just devastated about losing Todd to the forces of evil. She was questioning her worth as a social services worker and how a failure with Todd would affect her ability to help other people later.

"Todd sealed his own fate, Paige," Phoebe said. "There's nothing you can do to help him now."

"I don't believe that Todd has chosen evil." Determined to prove it, Paige positioned herself in Todd's line of fire. "But let's find out for sure. If he's the kind of person that can kill without hesitation or compunction, we'll know as soon as you take the freeze off, Piper."

"And let him zing you with the Darklighter death ray?" Piper eyed Paige narrowly. "Not."

Paige rolled her eyes. "I can orb, remember? If he shoots, I'm out of here in a flash—literally."

"We have to know," Phoebe said, "beyond a doubt."

"They're right, Piper," Leo said. "The boy's future—one way or another—depends on what he does next."

"Okay. Here goes. Ready?" When Paige nodded, Piper sighed, flexed her fingers, and waved her hand.

Although Paige was confident she could orb out ahead of an arrow, Phoebe was coiled to shove her out of the arrow's flight path if necessary. Even NASA had back-up systems and programmed redundancy. She held her breath when Todd twitched.

Paige stood her ground.

The wail of frustration and pain that had been frozen in Todd's throat echoed off the walls as he spun and shot the statue of the headless deer. He dropped the weapon and sagged.

Paige was at the boy's side in a heartbeat, wrapping her arms around him, cradling his head against her shoulder. "It's all right, Todd. It's over. Everything Scar said was a lie. Everything. You're okay, Todd. You're okay."

"I wasn't going to shoot you," Todd sobbed. "Honest, I wasn't."

"I know." Paige hushed him.

"So Todd *was* our innocent," Piper noted matter-of-factly.

"Looks that way," Leo said.

When a chunk of crumbling cement fell from the headless deer, Piper whirled and blew off a front leg.

"Piper!" Leo threw up his hands. "The threat is over."

"*This* threat is over." Piper shoved her hands in her pocket with a sheepish shrug, then laughed. "Gotcha!"

"Over except for a couple of poisonous loose ends." Phoebe pointed to the crossbow and arrow on the stones at Todd's feet.

"Ah, yes. We can't leave those lying around." Piper waved the boy to move back then flicked her fingers. The Darklighter weapons were obliterated in a flash of fire.

"We're still not done yet." Paige stepped back from Todd but kept a comforting arm around his shoulders. "We've still got to deal with Ray Marino."

"Do we have evidence of a crime?" Leo asked.

"That depends on whether Todd wants to testify against him," Paige said.

"I'll talk." Squaring his shoulders, Todd eased out from under Paige's arm. "That guy hates kids. He sold us out to Scar."

"We'd better find him before he makes a run for it then." Phoebe glanced around the courtyard. "How do we get into the house from here?"

"This way." Todd waved them to follow and headed for a set of large double doors.

Phoebe had to marveled at Todd's ability to bounce back after two days of extreme emotional pressure. She could only hope that the resilience he showed in the immediate situation would finally take root in his life. For five years, he had stubbornly refused to accept his mother's death and move on. Maybe being exposed to pure evil would help him put things in perspective. Once Todd realized that being happy would not betray his mom's memory, he could start living for the future instead of in the past.

"Bay Haven's board could hold a dynamite haunted house fundraiser down here," Piper observed as they moved into a narrow passageway.

"I'll mention it," Paige said, "provided the home stays open after Ray is brought up on charges."

Phoebe brought up the rear. The long corridor was lit by a single lightbulb and covered with spiderwebs. It ended in a large cellar that was used for laundry and storage.

"Do those stairs go into the kitchen?" Leo asked Todd as he took the lead.

Nodding, Todd fell into line behind Leo, Piper, and Paige. "I don't think Ray will be there." He whispered.

"Have the boys eaten already?" Paige whispered back, frowning.

"We, uh, split a sandwich a couple of hours ago." Todd sighed. "Ian and Tyrell decided to fight for it so they didn't get any."

"One sandwich for the four of you?" Phoebe asked.

"Are you serious?" Paige hissed, appalled.

Paige frowned. "If Ray wasn't feeding you properly, that's a violation—"

Leo waved Paige to silence as he opened the door at the top of the stairs. The kitchen was deserted, but the sound of angry male voices carried from the front of the house.

"Where are the other boys now?" Leo asked softly.

"Probably watching TV in the upstairs community room," Todd said.

The group moved with cautious stealth down the hall that led into the large entry foyer. From their discussions with Paige, Phoebe knew that a cook and a teacher were the only employees on the premises besides Ray and the gardener. It was impossible to tell how many of them were involved in the heated argument taking place in the office near the front door.

"Hadie!" Todd ran to a cat carrier on the floor and knelt to peer through the wire door. "Are you okay?"

The orange cat mewed.

Piper and Paige hung back as Leo entered the large library that doubled as an office. "Cole?"

Phoebe paused in the doorway, stunned. Cole

had Ray backed against a wall with his hand around his throat.

"Hi, Leo!" Cole's smiling glance flicked from the Whitelighter to a bank of surveillance monitors. "I caught our friend here making a run for it. Guess he didn't like the instant reply of the Darklighter's demise."

Phoebe stepped inside to look. A tape of Scar going down in flames was playing over and over in a continuous loop on the center monitor screen.

"What are you doing here, Cole?" Leo asked.

"When nobody answered a phone, I figured you were all out here and I came to help." Cole's grip on Ray's neck tightened when the wiry administrator struggled. Cole's smile brightened when he glanced back. "Hi, Phoebe."

"Hi." Phoebe replied.

"Is everyone else okay?" Cole asked. "Piper and Paige?"

"They're fine," Phoebe answered.

"Good. Then we don't need him." Cole drew a fist back and punched Ray in the jaw. Shaking his hand, he turned to Phoebe and frowned. "I thought you were going to call."

"Was I?" Phoebe grinned. All was well that ended well, and Cole wouldn't stay mad forever.

Chapter

13

"Hello!" Paige slammed the front door and hurried into the kitchen. "Where is everyone?"

"Out here, Paige!" Piper's voice carried through an open window. She smiled and waved a trowel. Wearing rolled up jeans, a plaid shirt, and a wide-brimmed straw hat, she looked like a country girl.

Phoebe sat in one of the plastic chairs, reading a book and sipping iced tea from a tall, frosty glass. She moved her sunglasses down her nose to peer over the upper rim and smiled. "Grab a cold one and join us, Paige!"

Paige dropped her bag on the counter and pulled a canned soda from the fridge on her way out the door. She stop dead in her tracks when she saw what Piper's green thumb had produced in the backyard. She had been so busy at work in the week since they had vanquished

Scar, she hadn't paid attention to the "farm," as Piper's garden was affectionately known among friends and family.

"What are those?" Paige stared.

"These?" Piper gestured at the tomato plants. Supported by wire cones and wooden stakes, the four-foot high, bushy plants were laden with ripe, red tomatoes the size of grapefruits. "Tomatoes."

"Those beauties are instant gratification plus." Paige popped the top of the soda and took a long drink. "I don't know what you used on those plants, Piper, but we've got to market that stuff."

"That's what I said." Phoebe sighed. "The Halliwell Growth Compost Company would have made us a small fortune."

"Except for the no-personal-gain clause in the rules of acceptable witch conduct," Piper said. "And that other little detail."

"What detail?" Paige was sure there had to be a loophole for folk fertilizer.

"I can't duplicate the recipe." Piper shrugged. "I used the first batch on the tomatoes and made more, but none of the next five batches has created super veggies."

"Apparently the 'Jack and the Beanstalk' effect is a one-time-only phenomenon." Phoebe took a sip of tea.

"Twice if the fairytale is fact and not fiction," Piper said.

"Well, that's a rotten shame." Shaking her head, Paige walked over to the chair beside Phoebe and sat. She propped her feet on a plastic crate holding small bags of the peat moss and organic soil mix Piper used for flowers.

"How'd it go with Todd?" Phoebe asked.

"Great!" Putting lost business opportunities out of her mind, Paige leaned forward. "His father is a gem. If Kari had tried to find Brian Jamieson when she was pregnant, she'd probably still be alive and happily married to him."

"At least you finally found him." Piper exchanged her trowel for a basket and began picking the ripest tomatoes.

"Along with a current wife that's a priceless gem too," Phoebe added.

"Would you believe?" Paige was still amazed at her luck in tracking down Brian and Kelly Jamieson. After eight years of marriage, the childless couple had decided to adopt six months before. She had found their application in the county database. Brian had had no idea he had a son, and when he found out, he and his lovely wife had welcomed Todd into their hearts and home.

"They are one big happy family now," Paige said, raising her soda in a toast.

"The cat, too?" Phoebe cringed as though that would ward off bad news.

Todd had latched onto the stray cat the day they had rescued him from Scar. After what he'd

been through, no one had had the heart to take
Hadie away from him.

"I was pretty sure Todd's new parents would
accept the cat," Paige said.

Phoebe clinked her glass against Paige's can.
"Here's to happily-ever-afters. May we have
bunches more."

"I'll second that." Piper held up a tomato and
took a juicy bite.

"And may my visions be fog-free for a very
long time." Phoebe shuddered. "The mist-and-
stone effect is way too hard on the nerves!"

Paige settled back with a definitive sense of
well-being. She would continue to regard
Darklighters with apprehension, but her deep-
seated dread had been conquered. The
Whitelighter killers were just another underworld danger she would have to face and defeat
in her life as a Charmed One.

Todd would eventually conquer his inner
demons too. Although he wasn't quite as enthusiastic about his new circumstances as his parents, Hank, and the cat, Paige was certain that he
would adjust and thrive. No one knew better
than she that the bond of blood and family love
was powerful and enduring.

A warm glow of contentment washed over
Paige as she glanced at Piper and Phoebe.

No matter how long it takes to find it.

About The Author

Diana G. Gallagher lives in Florida with her husband, Marty Burke, four dogs, seven cats, and a cranky parrot. Before becoming a full-time writer, she made her living in a variety of occupations, including hunter seat equitation instructor, folk musician, and fantasy artist. Best known for her hand-colored prints depicting the doglike activities of *Woof: The House Dragon*, she won a Hugo Award for Best Fan Artist in 1988.

Diana's first science fiction novel, *The Alien Dark*, was published in 1990. Since then, she has written more than forty novels for Pocket Books in several series for all age groups, including Star Trek for middle readers; Sabrina, The Teenage Witch; Charmed; Buffy the Vampire Slayer; The Secret World Of Alex Mack; Are You Afraid of the Dark; and Salem's Tails.